She was not going to marry Patrick Devlin!

He was mad. Completely. Utterly insane!

His mouth quirked with amusement as he saw those emotions flashing across her expressive face. "A month, Lilli," he told her softly. "You will be my wife within the month."

Lilli looked up at him frowning; his gaze was enigmatic now. He sounded so sure of himself, so calmly certain....

CAROLE MORTIMER says: "I was born in England, the youngest of three children—I have two older brothers. I started writing in 1978, and have now written over ninety books for Harlequin Presents®.

"I have four sons—Matthew, Joshua, Timothy and Peter—and a bearded collie dog called Merlyn. I'm in a very happy relationship with Peter Senior; we're best friends as well as lovers, which is probably the best recipe for a successful relationship. We live on the Isle of Man."

Books by Carole Mortimer

Carole Mortimer

Married by Christmas

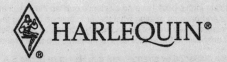

HARLEQUIN®

TORONTO • NEW YORK • LONDON
AMSTERDAM • PARIS • SYDNEY • HAMBURG
STOCKHOLM • ATHENS • TOKYO • MILAN • MADRID
PRAGUE • WARSAW • BUDAPEST • AUCKLAND

ISBN 0-373-11995-X

MARRIED BY CHRISTMAS

First North American Publication 1998.

This edition published by arrangement with Harlequin Books S.A.

® and TM are trademarks of the publisher. Trademarks indicated with
® are registered in the United States Patent and Trademark Office, the
Canadian Trade Marks Office and in other countries.

Printed in U.S.A.

CHAPTER ONE

'WHO *is* that gorgeous-looking man over there?' Sally gushed eagerly at Lilli's side.

Until that moment, Lilli had been staring sightlessly at a barman across the room as he quickly and efficiently served drinks to the multitude of people attending what had so far been a pretty boring party.

Or maybe it wasn't the party that was boring; maybe it was just Lilli who felt slightly out of sync with the rest of the people here: if the babble of noise was anything to go by they were having such a good time.

She hadn't attended a party like this in such a long while, and so much had happened in the preceding months. Once upon a time, she acknowledged, she would have thought this was a great party too, would have been at the centre of whatever was going on, but tonight—well, tonight she felt like a total outsider, rather as the only sober person in a room full of inebriates must feel. Except she had already consumed several glasses of champagne herself, so that wasn't the reason she felt so out of touch with this crowd with which she had once spent so much time.

As for gorgeous men, the house was full of them— gorgeous and rich. When Geraldine Simms threw a party, this a pre-Christmas one, only the rich and beautiful were invited to attend, in their hundreds. Geraldine's house, in a fashionable part of London, was as huge and prepossessing as its neighbours, and tonight it was bursting at the seams with bejewelled women and handsome men.

Lilli dragged her gaze away from the efficient barman, obviously hired for the evening. It was time she looked away anyway—the man had obviously noticed her attention several minutes ago, and, from the speculative look in his eyes, believed he had made a conquest! He couldn't have been further from the truth; the last thing Lilli was interested in was a fling with any man, let alone someone as transient as a hired barman!

'What gorgeous man?' she asked Sally without interest. Sally was the one who had persuaded her to come in the first place, on the basis that a Geraldine Simms party, an event that only happened twice a year, was a party not to be missed.

'Over by the door— Oh, damn it, he's disappeared again!' Sally frowned her irritation. She was a petite blonde, with a beauty that could stop a man in his tracks, the black dress she almost wore doing little to forestall this.

Lilli had met her several years ago, during the usual round of parties, and, because neither of them had any interest in becoming permanently entangled with any of the handsome men they encountered, they often found themselves spending the evening together laughing at some of the antics of the other women around them as they cast out their nets and secured some unsuspecting man for the evening. Rather a cruel occupation, really, but it had got Lilli and Sally through many a tedious occasion.

'He must be gorgeous if you've taken an interest,' Lilli said dryly, attracting more than her own fair share of admiring glances as she stood tall and slender next to Sally, her hair long and straight to her waist, as black as a raven's wing, eyes cool and green in a gaminely beautiful face, the strapless above-knee-length red dress that she wore clinging to the perfection of her body. Her legs were long and shapely, still tanned from the summer months, the red high-heeled shoes she wore only adding to her height—and to the impression of unobtainable aloofness that she had practised to perfection over the years.

'Oh, he is,' Sally assured her, still searching the crowd for the object of her interest. 'He makes all the other men here look like callow, narcissistic youths. He— Oh, damn,' she swore impatiently. 'Oh, well,' she sighed, turning back to Lilli with a rueful grimace. 'That was fun while it lasted!' She sipped her champagne.

Lilli's eyes widened. 'You've given up already?' She sounded surprised because she was. On the few occasions she had known Sally to take an interest in a man, she hadn't given up until she had got him! And, as far as Lilli was aware, her friend had always succeeded...

'Had to.' Sally grimaced her disappointment, taking another sip of her champagne. 'Unobtainable.'

'You mean he's married,' Lilli said knowingly.

Sally arched her brows. 'I'm sorry to say that hasn't always been a deterrent in the past.' She shook her head. 'No, he belongs to Gerry,' she explained disappointedly. 'As far as I'm aware, no woman has ever taken one of our hostess's men and lived to tell the tale. And I'm too young to die!'

Lilli laughed huskily at her friend's woebegone expression. Sally was exaggerating, of course, although Geraldine's succession of lovers was legendary. In fact, Lilli doubted there were too many men in this room the beautiful Geraldine Simms hadn't been involved with at some time or other during the last few years. But at least she seemed to stay good friends with them, which had to say something about the bubbling effervescence of their hostess!

Sally glanced across the room again. 'But he is *so* gorgeous…' she said longingly.

Lilli gave a shake of her head. 'Okay, I give up; where is he?' She turned to look for the man who was so attractive that Sally seemed to be about to throw caution to the wind and challenge Gerry for him, on the other woman's home ground, no less!

'Over there.' Sally nodded to the far side of the elegantly furnished room. 'Standing next to Gerry near the window.'

Sally continued to give an exact description of the gorgeous man but Lilli was no longer listening to her, having already located the intimately engrossed couple, feeling the blood drain from her cheeks as she easily spotted the man standing so arrogantly self-assured at Geraldine's side.

No!

Not him. Not here. Not with *her*!

Oh, God…! How could he? How dared he?

'Isn't he just—? I say, Lilli, you've gone very pale all of a sudden.' Sally looked at her concernedly.

Pale? She was surprised she hadn't gone grey, shocked she was still standing on legs that seemed to be shaking so badly her knees were knocking together, surprised she wasn't screaming, *accusing*. What was *he* doing here? And so obviously with Geraldine Simms, a woman with the reputation of a man-eater.

'Are you feeling okay?' Sally touched her arm worriedly.

She wasn't feeling at all, seemed to have gone completely numb. It wasn't an emotion she was unfamiliar with, but she had never thought he would be the one to deal her such a blow.

Oh, God, she had to get out of here, away from the noise, away from *them*!

'I'm fine, Sally,' she told her friend stiltedly, the smile she forced not quite managing to curve her lips. 'I—I think I've had enough for one night. It's my first time out for months,' she babbled. 'I'm obviously out of practice. I—I'll call you.' She put her champagne glass down on the nearest available table. 'We'll have lunch.'

Sally looked totally bewildered by Lilli's sudden urgency to be gone. 'But it's only eleven-thirty!'

And the party would go on until almost morning. In the past Lilli would probably have been among the last to leave. But not tonight. She had to get out of here now. She had to!

'I'll call you, Sally,' she promised distantly, turning to stumble across the room, muttering her apologies as she bumped into people on the way, blind to where she was going, just needing to escape.

She had a jacket somewhere, she remembered. It was in a room at the back of the house. And she didn't want to leave without it, didn't want to have to come back to this house again to collect it. She didn't want to ever have to see Geraldine Simms again. Not ever!

Where had they stored the coats? Every room she looked in appeared to be empty. One of them turned out not to be as empty as it at first appeared, a young couple in there taking advantage of the sofa to make love. But there were no coats.

She would just abandon her damn coat in a minute, would send someone over tomorrow for it, would just have to hope that it was still here.

She thrust open another door, deciding that if this

room proved as fruitless as the others she would quietly
leave and find herself a taxi.

'Oh!' She gasped as she realised she had walked into
what must be the main kitchen of the house. It wasn't
empty. Not that there were any chefs rushing around
preparing the food for the numerous guests. No, all the
food, put out so deliciously on plates in the dining-room,
had been provided by caterers.

A man sat at a long oak table in the middle of the
room, his dark evening suit and snowy white shirt, with
red bow-tie, tagging him as part of the elegant gathering
in the main part of the house. Yet he sat alone in the
kitchen, strong hands nursing what looked to be a glass
of red wine, the open bottle on the table beside him, the
only light in the room a single spotlight over the Aga.

But Lilli could see the man well enough, his dark,
overlong hair with distinguished strands of grey at the
temples, grey, enigmatic eyes in a face that might have
been carved from granite, all sharp angles and hard-
hewn features. From the way his long legs stretched out
beneath the table, he was a very tall man, well over six
feet, if Lilli had to guess. She would put his age in the
late thirties.

She also knew, from that very first glance, that she
had never seen him before!

She really was very much out of touch with the party
scene! Once upon a time she would have known all the
other guests at any occasion she went to, which was
ultimately the reason they had become so boring to attend. But tonight there were at least two men present
that she hadn't encountered at one of these parties before—one she didn't know at all, the other she most
certainly did!

Her mouth tightened at her thoughts. 'I'm sorry to

have disturbed you,' she told the man distractedly, turning to leave.

'Not at all,' the man drawled in a weary voice. 'It's quite pleasant to meet another refugee from that free-for-all out there!'

Lilli turned slowly back to him, dark brows raised. 'You aren't enjoying the party?'

His mouth quirked into a humourless smile, and he took a swallow of the wine before answering. 'Not particularly,' he dismissed disgustedly. 'If I had known—!' He picked up the bottle and refilled his glass, turning back to Lilli and raising the bottle in her direction. 'Can I offer you some wine? It's from Gerry's private stock,' he explained temptingly. 'Much preferable to that champagne being served out there.' He waved the bottle in the direction of the front of the house.

Gerry... Only Geraldine's really close friends shortened her name in that way. He also knew where Geraldine kept her cellar of wine.

Lilli looked at the man with new interest. He obviously was—or had been—a close friend of Geraldine Simms. And, while Geraldine might remain on good terms with her ex-lovers, she certainly didn't give them up to another woman easily...

Lilli entered the kitchen fully, aware of the man's gaze on her as she moved across the dimly lit room, able to tell by the cool assessment in those pale grey eyes that he liked what he saw. 'I would love some wine,' she accepted as she sat down at the table, not opposite him but next to him, pushing a long swathe of her dark hair over her shoulder as she did so, turning to look at him, green eyes dark, a smile curving lips coloured the same red as her dress. 'Thank you,' she added huskily.

'Good.' He nodded his satisfaction with her answer, standing up to get a second glass.

Now it was Lilli's turn to watch him. She had been right about his height; he must be at least six feet four, the cut of his suit doing nothing to hide the powerfully muscled body beneath. It also did nothing to mask his obvious contempt for these elegant trappings of civilised company!

She had no doubt that Sally would also have described him as gorgeous!

Her smile faded somewhat as she vividly brought to mind that image of the other man Sally had called gorgeous tonight; her last vision had been of Geraldine Simms draped decoratively across him as the two of them talked softly together.

'Thank you,' she told the man as he sat down beside her to pour her wine, picking up the glass when it was filled to swallow a grateful gulp. She could instantly feel the warmth of the wine inside her, merging with the glasses of champagne she had already consumed.

'Patrick Devlin.' The man held out his hand.

'Lilli.' She shook his hand, liking its cool strength, his name meaning absolutely nothing to her.

He raised dark brows, still retaining his light hold on her hand. 'Just Lilli?'

Her gaze met his, seeing a wealth of experience in those grey depths. Some of that experience had been with Geraldine Simms, she felt sure. 'Just Lilli,' she nodded, sensing his interest in her. And she intended to keep that interest...

'Well, Just Lilli...' He slowly released her hand, although his gaze still easily held hers. 'As we're both bored with this party, what do you suggest we do with ourselves for the rest of the evening?' He quirked mocking lips.

She laughed softly, well versed in the art of seduction herself. 'What do you suggest we do?' she encouraged softly.

He turned back to sit with his elbows resting on the table, sipping his wine. 'Well...we could count how many patterned tiles there are on the wall over there.' He nodded to the wall opposite.

Lilli didn't so much as glance at them. 'I have no interest in counting tiles, patterned or otherwise,' she returned dryly, drinking some of her own wine. He was right—this wine was much nicer than champagne. It was taking away the numbness she had felt earlier, too.

'No? Oh, well.' He shrugged at the playful shake of her head, refilling her glass. 'We could swap life stories?'

'Definitely not!' There was an edge of bitterness to her laugh this time.

He pursed his lips thoughtfully. 'You're probably right,' he said. 'We could bake a cake? We're certainly in the right place for it!' He looked about them.

'Can you cook?' Lilli prompted; he didn't look as if he knew one end of a cooker—or Aga!—from the other!

He grinned at her, showing very white and even teeth—and unlike most of the men here tonight, she would swear that he'd had none of them capped. 'No one has yet complained about my toast,' he drawled. 'And I've been told I pour a mean glass of orange juice!'

She nodded as he gave her the answer she had expected. 'And a mean glass of wine.' She raised her glass as if in a salute to him.

He poured the last of the wine into her glass. 'I'll open another bottle.' He stood up, moving confidently about the kitchen, walking to the cupboard at the back of the room, emerging triumphantly seconds later with a second bottle of the same wine.

Which he then proceeded to open deftly, refilling his own glass before sitting down next to Lilli once again. 'Your turn. To make some suggestions,' he elaborated huskily at her questioning look.

His words themselves were suggestive, but at this particular moment Lilli didn't care. She was actually enjoying herself, and after the shock she had received earlier this evening that was something in itself.

'Let me see...' She made a show of giving it some thought, happily playing along with the game. 'Do you play chess?'

'Tolerably,' he replied.

'Hmm. Draughts?'

'A champion,' he assured her confidently. 'That's the one with the black and white discs—'

'Not draughts, either,' Lilli laughed, green eyes glowing, her cheeks warm, whether from the effect of the wine and champagne, or their verbal flirtation, she wasn't really sure.

And she didn't care, either. This man was a special friend of Geraldine Simms', she was sure of it, and at this moment she had one hundred per cent of his attention. Wonderful!

'Snakes and ladders?' she suggested lightly.

'Yes...' he answered slowly. 'Although my sister always said I cheated when we played as children; I used to go up the snakes and down the ladders!'

Lilli laughed again. Either the man really was funny, or else the wine was taking effect; either way, this was the most fun she had had in a long time. 'I used to do that too,' she confided, lightly touching his arm, instantly feeling the steely strength beneath his jacket. 'And there's no way we can play if we both cheat!'

'True,' he agreed, suddenly very close, his face mere inches away from hers now. 'You know, Just Lilli, there's one game I have an idea we're both good at— and at which neither of us cheats!' His voice was mesmerisingly low now, his aftershave faintly elusive, but at the same time completely masculine. 'What do you say to the two of us—?'

'Patrick!' A feminine voice, slightly raised with impatience, interrupted him. 'Why aren't you at the party?'

He held Lilli's eyes for several seconds longer, a promise in his own, lightly squeezing her hand as it still rested on his arm, before turning to face the source of that feminine impatience. 'Because I prefer to be here,' he answered firmly. 'And, luckily for me, so does Lilli.'

'Lilli…?' The woman sounded startled now.

So much so that Lilli finally turned to look at her too. Geraldine Simms! She looked far from pleased to see the two of them sitting so close together, Patrick's hand still resting slightly possessively on Lilli's.

Lilli looked coldly at the other woman. 'Geraldine,' she greeted her hardly.

'I didn't realise you were here,' Geraldine said faintly.

She could easily have guessed that! 'Sally Walker telephoned me earlier and persuaded me to come with her.' Lilli finished abruptly, 'Wonderful party,' her sarcasm barely veiled.

'So wonderful Lilli and I were just about to leave.' Patrick stood up, lightly pulling Lilli to her feet beside him, his arm moving about the slenderness of her waist now. 'Weren't we,' he prompted.

As far as Lilli was aware—no, but it did seem like an excellent idea.

She turned her head slightly to give Geraldine a triumphant look. 'Yes, we were just about to leave,' she agreed brightly.

'But—' Geraldine looked flustered, not at all her usually confident self. 'Patrick, you can't leave!' She looked at him beseechingly, not at all certain of herself—or him.

His arm tightened about Lilli's waist. 'Watch me,' he stated determinedly.

'But—' Geraldine wrung her hands together. 'Patrick, I threw this party partly for you—'

'I hate parties, you know that.' There was a hard edge to his voice that hadn't been there when he'd flirted with Lilli. 'I'll come back tomorrow when all of this is over. In the meantime, I intend booking into a hotel for the night. Unless Lilli has any other ideas?' he added, looking at her with raised brows.

'Just Lilli' had realised, from the conversation between these two, that the original plan must have been for Patrick to spend the night here. And, considering Geraldine's intimacy with the man she had been draped over in the other room, that was no mean feat in itself; what did this woman do, line them up in relays? Whatever, Patrick had obviously decided he would rather spend the night with her, though the house she shared in Mayfair with her father was not the place for her to take him; she felt hurt and betrayed, but not *that* hurt and betrayed!

'A hotel sounds fine,' she accepted with bravado, green eyes challenging as she looked across the room at Geraldine.

The other woman's stare relaxed slightly as she met that challenge. 'Lilli, don't do something you'll regret,' she cautioned gently.

Geraldine knew she had seen the two of *them* together,

knew why she was doing this! All the better; there was no satisfaction in revenge if the person targeted was unaware of it...!

Lilli turned slightly into Patrick's body, resting her head against the hardness of his chest. 'I'm sure Patrick will make sure I don't regret a thing,' she said huskily.

'Lilli—'

'Gerry, just butt out, will you?' Patrick told her impatiently. 'Go and find your ageing lover and leave Lilli and me to get on with our lives. I'm not a monster intent on seducing an innocent, and you aren't the girl's mother, for goodness' sake,' he added disgustedly.

Lilli looked at the other woman with pure venom in her eyes; she had never disliked anyone as much as she did Geraldine Simms at that moment. 'Yes, Geraldine,' she said flatly. 'Please go back to your lover; I'm sure he must be wondering where you are.'

'We'll go out the back way,' Patrick suggested lightly. 'Unless you want to fight your way out through the chaos?'

'No, the back way is fine.' Her coat didn't matter any more; no doubt it would be returned to her in time!

'Patrick!' Geraldine had crossed the room to stop them at the door, a restraining hand on Patrick's arm now. 'I realise you're angry with me right now, but please don't—'

'I'm not angry with you, Gerry,' he cut in contemptuously. 'No one has any ties on you; they never had!' His face was cold as he looked down at her.

'This isn't important just now,' the beautiful redhead dismissed impatiently. 'Anyone but Lilli, Patrick,' she groaned.

So the woman did have a conscience, after all! Unless, of course, she just didn't want Lilli, in particular, walking off with one of her men...? In the circumstances, that was probably closer to the truth.

'Please don't worry on my account, Geraldine.' Lilli deliberately used the other woman's full name. The two of them had never been particularly close in the past, although Lilli did usually call her Gerry; but after this evening she hoped they would never meet again. 'I know exactly what I'm doing,' she affirmed.

Geraldine looked at Lilli searchingly for several long seconds. 'I don't think you do.' She shook her head slowly. 'And I'm absolutely positive you don't, Patrick,' she added firmly. 'Lilli is—'

'Could we leave now, Patrick?' Lilli turned to him, open flirtation in the dark green of her eyes. 'Before I decide snakes and ladders is preferable!'

He looked at her admiringly. 'We're leaving, Gerry,' he told the other woman decisively. 'Now.'

'But—'

'Now, Gerry,' he insisted, opening the back door for Lilli to precede him. 'Enjoy your party,' he called over his shoulder, his arm once more about Lilli's waist as they stepped out into the cold December evening.

The blast of icy cold air was like a slap on the face, and Lilli could feel her head swimming from the amount of champagne and wine she had drunk during the evening. In fact, she suddenly felt decidedly light-headed.

'Steady.' Patrick's arm tightened about her waist as he held her beside him. 'My car is just over here. Don't you have a coat?' He frowned as she shivered from the cold while he unlocked the doors of his sleek black sports car.

She suddenly couldn't remember whether she had a coat or not. In fact, she was having trouble putting two thoughts together inside her head!

She gave a laugh as he opened the car door for her to get in, showing a long expanse of shapely leg as she dropped down into the low passenger seat. 'I'm sure you'll help me to get warm once we reach the hotel,' she told him seductively.

His mouth quirked. 'I'll do my best, Just Lilli,' he assured her, the promise in his voice unmistakable.

Lilli leant her head back against the seat as he closed her door to move around the car and get in behind the wheel. What was she doing here…? Oh, yes, she was getting away from Geraldine and him!

'Any preference on hotels?' Patrick glanced at her as he turned on the ignition.

Hotels? Why were they going to a hotel…? Oh, yes…this man was going to make love to her.

She shook her head, instantly wishing she hadn't as it began to spin once again. 'You choose,' she said weakly.

She wasn't actually going to be sick, was she?

God, she hoped not. Although she had no idea where they were going as Patrick turned the car out onto the road. And at that moment she didn't care either. Nothing mattered at the moment. Not her. Not him. Not Geraldine Simms!

'All right?' Patrick reached out to squeeze her hand reassuringly.

She didn't think she would ever be 'all right' again. She had felt as if her world had shattered three months ago; tonight it felt as if it had ended completely.

'Fine,' she answered as if from a long way away. 'Just take me somewhere private and make love to me.'

'Oh, I intend to, Just Lilli. I intend to.'

Lilli sat back with her eyes closed, wishing at that moment for total oblivion, not just a few hours in Patrick Devlin's arms…

CHAPTER TWO

'YOUR jacket.' The garment was thrown over the back of a dining-room chair.

Lilli didn't move, didn't even raise her head. She wasn't sure that she could!

She had been sitting here at the dining-table for the last hour, just drinking strong, unsweetened black coffee; the smell of food on the serving plates sitting on the side board had made her feel nauseous, so she had asked for them to be taken away. There was no one else here to eat it, anyway. At least, there hadn't been...

'Did you hear what I said?'

'I heard you!' She winced as the sound of her own voice made the thumping in her head even louder. 'I heard you,' she repeated softly, her voice almost a whisper now. But it still sounded too loud for her sensitive ears!

'Well?'

He wasn't going to leave it at that. She should have known that he wouldn't. But all she really wanted to do, now that her head had at least stopped spinning, was to crawl into bed and sleep for twenty-four hours.

Fat chance!

'Lilli!' The impatience deepened in his voice.

At last she raised her head from where it had been resting in her hands as she stared down into her coffee cup, pushing back the dark thickness of her hair to look up at him with studied determination.

'My God, Lilli!' her father gasped disbelievingly. 'You look terrible!'

'Thank you!' Her smile was merely a caricature of one, even her facial muscles seeming to hurt.

She knew exactly how she looked, had recoiled from her own reflection in the mirror earlier this morning. Her eyes were a dull green, bruises from lack of sleep visible beneath them, her face chalk-white. Her tangled hair she had managed to smooth into some sort of order with her fingers, but the overall impression, she knew, was not good. It wasn't helped by the fact that she still had on the revealing red dress she had worn to the party the night before. A fact Grimes, the family butler, had definitely noted when she'd arrived back here by taxi an hour ago!

But if her father thought she looked bad now he should have seen her a couple of hours ago, when she'd first woken up; then she hadn't even been wearing the red dress! And the rich baritone voice of Patrick Devlin had been coming from the bathroom as he'd sung while he took a shower...!

Her father dropped down heavily into the chair opposite her. 'What were you thinking of, Lilli?' He looked at her searchingly. 'Or were you just not thinking at all?' he added with regret.

He knew; she could tell by the expression in his eyes that he did. Of course he knew; Geraldine would have told him!

Because her father had been the man at Geraldine Simms' side last night, the gorgeous man that Sally had referred to so interestedly, the man Geraldine had been draped over so intimately, her 'ageing lover', as Patrick had called him.

'Were *you*?' Lilli challenged insultingly. 'Yes, I saw

you last night,' she scorned as a guarded look came over
her father's handsome face. 'With Geraldine Simms,'
she continued accusingly, so angry she didn't care about
the pounding in her head at that moment. 'But I suppose
you call her Gerry.' Her top lip curled back contemptuously. 'All her *intimate* friends do!'

He drew in a harshly controlling breath. 'And is that
why you did what you did?' he asked flatly. 'Went off
with a man you had only just met? A man you obviously
spent the night with,' he added as he looked pointedly
at her dress.

'And what about you?' Lilli accused emotionally. 'I
don't need to ask where *you* spent the night. Or with
whom!' She was furiously angry, but at the same time
tears of pain glistened in her eyes.

Her father reached out to touch her hand, but she drew
back as if she had been burnt. 'You don't understand,
Lilli,' he told her in a hurt voice. 'You—'

'Oh, I understand only too well.' She stood up so
suddenly, her chair fell over behind her with a loud clat-
ter, but neither of them took any notice of it as their
green eyes locked. 'You spent last night in the bed of a
woman everyone knows to be a man-eating flirt, a
woman who has been involved with numerous men since
her brief marriage—and equally quick divorce!—five
years ago. And with my mother, your wife, barely cold
in her grave!' She glared across the table at him, her
breathing shallow and erratic in her agitation, her hands
clenched into fists at her sides.

For that was what hurt the most about all this. After
a long illness, her mother had died three months ago—
and now her father was intimately involved with one of
the biggest flirts in London!

It was an insult to her mother's memory. It was—it

was— God, the pain last night of seeing her father with another woman—with that woman in particular!—had been almost more than she could bear.

Her father looked as if she had physically hit him, his face as pale as her own, the likeness between them even more noticeable during those seconds. Lilli had always been so proud of her father, had adored him as a child, admired him as an adult, had always loved the fact that she looked so much like him, her hair as dark as his.

Now she wished she looked like anyone else but him—because at this particular moment she hated him!

'You're right, Father; I don't understand,' she told him coldly as she rose and walked away from him. 'But then, I don't think I particularly want to.'

'Lilli, did you spend the night with Patrick Devlin?'

She stopped at the door, her back still towards him. Then, swallowing hard, she turned to face him, her head held back defiantly. 'Yes, I did,' she told him starkly.

He frowned. 'You went to bed with him?'

Lilli stared at her parent woodenly. She had woken up in a hotel bedroom this morning, wearing only her lace panties, with Patrick Devlin singing in the adjoining bathroom as he took a shower, the other side of the double bed showing signs of someone having slept there, the pillow indented, the sheet tangled; so it was probably a fair assumption that she had been to bed with him!

But the real truth of the matter was she didn't actually remember, couldn't recall anything of the night before from the moment she had closed her eyes in the car—and even some of the events before that were a bit hazy!

Her mouth tightened stubbornly. 'What if I did? I'm over twenty-one.' Just! 'And a free agent.' Definitely that, since the end of her engagement. She had barely been out of the house during the last six months—which was the reason the champagne and wine she'd drunk last night had hit her so strongly, she was sure. At least, that was what she had told herself this morning when she'd finally managed to open her eyes and face the day. 'Who was I hurting?' she added challengingly.

Her father gave a weary sigh, shaking his head. 'Well, I believe the intention was to hurt me. But the person you've hurt the most is yourself. Lilli, do you have any idea who Patrick Devlin is?'

Why should she? As her father had already said, she had only met the man last night. And her nonsensical conversation with Patrick in the kitchen had told her nothing about him, except that he had a sense of humour. But then, she had told him nothing about herself either, was 'Just Lilli' as far as he was concerned. She never expected to see or hear from him again!

'I only wanted to go to bed with him, not hear his life story!' she scorned dismissively.

Her father drew a harsh breath. 'Perhaps if you had done the latter, and not the former, this conversation wouldn't be taking place. In fact, I'm sure it wouldn't,' he rasped abruptly. 'You really don't have any idea who he is?'

'Why do you keep harping on about the man?' She snapped her impatience. 'He isn't important—'

'Oh, but he is,' her father cut in softly.

'Not to me.' She gave a firm shake of her head, wincing as she did so.

She just wanted to forget about Patrick Devlin. Last night she had behaved completely out of character, mostly because, as her father had guessed, she wanted to hit out at him. But also at Geraldine Simms. Well, she had done that—more than done that if her father's reaction was anything to go by!—and now she just wanted to forget it had ever happened. She couldn't even remember half of last night's events, so it shouldn't be that hard to do!

'Oh, yes, Lilli, he is important to you too.' Her father nodded grimly. 'Patrick Devlin is the Chairman of Paradise Bank.'

She thought back to the man she had met last night in Geraldine Simms' kitchen—she couldn't count this morning; she had left the hotel before he'd stopped singing and emerged from the bathroom! She remembered a tall, handsome man, with slightly overlong dark hair, and laughter in his deep grey eyes. He hadn't looked anything like a banker.

She shrugged. 'So? Is he married, with a dozen children; is that the problem?' Although if he were he must have a very understanding wife, to have gone off to a party on his own and then have felt no compunction about staying out all night. No...somehow she didn't think he was married.

Her father gave a sigh at the mockery in her tone. 'Okay, let's leave that part alone for a while. Do you know what else he is, Lilli?'

'A Liberal Democrat,' she taunted.

'Oh, very funny!' Her father, a staunch Conservative voter, wasn't in the least amused at her continued levity.

'Look, Father, I don't—'

'And will you stop calling me "Father" in that judgemental tone?' he bit out tautly.

'I'm sorry, but you just don't seem like "Daddy" to me at the moment,' she told him in a pained voice, unable to look at him at that moment, too.

Her father had always been there for her in the past, she had always been 'Daddy's little girl', and now he suddenly seemed like a stranger...

'I'm really sorry you feel that way, Lilli.' He spoke gently. 'It wasn't meant to be this way.'

'I'm not even going to ask what you mean by that remark,' she said scathingly, turning towards the door once again.

'I haven't finished yet, Lilli—'

'But I have!' She swung round, eyes flashing deeply green. 'To be honest, I'm not sure I can listen to any more of this without being sick!' This time she did turn and walk out the door, her head held high.

'He's Geraldine's brother,' her father called after her. 'Patrick Devlin is Geraldine's older brother!'

She faltered only slightly, and then she just kept on walking, her legs moving automatically, that numbness she had known the night before thankfully creeping over her once again.

'Where are you going?' Her father now stood at the bottom of the stairs she had half ascended.

'To bed,' she told him flatly. 'To sleep.' For a million years, if she was lucky!

'This mess will still be here when you wake up, Lilli,' her father told her fiercely. '*I'll* still be here!'

She didn't answer him, didn't even glance at him, continuing up to her bedroom, closing the door firmly behind her, deliberately keeping her mind blank as she threw off the clothes she had worn last night, not even bothering to put on a nightgown before climbing in between the sheets of her bed, pulling the covers up over the top of her head, willing herself to go to sleep.

And when she woke up maybe she would find the last twelve hours had been a nightmare...!

Geraldine Simms' brother!

She didn't know what time it was, how long she had

slept, only that she had woken suddenly, sitting up in the bed, her eyes wide as that terrible truth pounded in her brain.

Patrick Devlin wasn't a past or present lover of Geraldine Simms, but her *brother*!

No wonder he had been so familiar with the house, with where the wine was kept. And he hadn't been going to spend the night there with Geraldine, but was obviously her guest at her house during his visit to London.

Lilli had thought she was being so clever, that she was walking away with a prize taken from under Geraldine's nose. But all the time Patrick was the woman's brother! No wonder Geraldine had tried to stop the two of them leaving together; considering her own involvement with Lilli's father, any relationship between Lilli and her brother was a complication she could well do without!

Lilli had been to bed with the enemy…!

But she wasn't involved with Patrick Devlin, had no 'relationship' with him; one night in bed together did not a relationship make!

One night in bed…

And she didn't even remember it, she inwardly groaned. But Patrick had been singing quite happily to himself in the shower this morning, so he obviously did!

With the exception of her ex-fiancé, she had spent the majority of the last four years ignoring the obvious advances of the 'beautiful men' she met at parties, not even aware of the less obvious ones. But in a single night she had wiped all of that out by going to bed with the one man she should have stayed well away from.

Her father was right—this was a mess!

She fell back against the pillows, her eyes closed. A

million years of sleep couldn't undo what she had done last night.

Her only consolation—and it was a very slight one!—was that she was sure Patrick had been involved in a conversation with his sister this morning very similar to the one she'd had with her father. She wouldn't be 'Just Lilli' to Patrick any more, but Elizabeth Bennett, daughter of Richard Bennett, of Bennett International Hotels, the current man in Geraldine's life. No doubt her identity as the daughter of his sister's 'ageing lover' had come as much of a shock to him as it had to her to realise he was Geraldine's brother.

Lilli opened her eyes, her expression thoughtful now. Patrick hadn't seemed any more pleased than she was at his sister's choice of lover, which meant he wouldn't be too eager ever to meet the lover's daughter again, either. Which meant she could forget the whole sorry business.

End of mess.

Of course it was.

Now if she could just make her father see sense over this ridiculous involvement with Geraldine Simms—

She turned towards the door as a knock sounded on it. She hadn't left instructions that she wasn't to be disturbed, but even so she was irritated at the intrusion. 'Yes?' she prompted impatiently, getting out of bed to pull on her robe.

'There's someone downstairs waiting to see you, Miss Lilli, and—'

The young maid broke off in surprise as Lilli wrenched open the door. 'There's someone to see you,' the maid repeated awkwardly.

'What time is it?' Lilli frowned, totally disoriented after her daytime sleep.

'Three-thirty,' Emily provided, a girl not much

younger than Lilli herself. 'Would you like me to s
tea to you and your visitor?'

She wasn't in the mood to receive visitors, let alone
sit and have tea with them. 'I don't think so, thank you,'
she replied distractedly. 'Who is it?' She frowned.

'A Mr Devlin,' Emily told her chattily. 'I asked him
to wait in the small sitting-room—'

'Devlin!' Lilli repeated forcefully, causing the young
maid to look alarmed all over again. 'Did you say a Mr
Devlin, Emily?' Her thoughts raced.

Patrick was here? So much for her thinking he
wouldn't ever want to see her again either once he realised who she was!

'Yes.' The young girl's face was alight with infatua-
tion—all the evidence Lilli needed that indeed it was the
handsome Patrick Devlin downstairs.

Thinking back to the way he had looked last night—
tall, and so elegantly handsome—she found it easy to
see how a woman's breath could be taken away just to
look at him. And she had just spent the night with him!

Lilli drew in a sharp breath. 'Please tell him I'll be
down in a few minutes.' Once she was dressed. His last
memory of her must be of her wearing only cream lace
panties; she intended the memory he took away of her
today to be quite different!

It took more than the few minutes she had said to don
a black sweater, fitted black trousers, apply a light make-
up to hide the pallor of her face, and to braid her long
hair into a loose plait down her spine. But at least when
she looked in the mirror at her reflection she was satis-
fied with the result—cool and elegant.

Nevertheless, she took a deep breath before entering
the room where Patrick Devlin waited for her. She had
no idea what he was doing here—didn't a woman walk-

ing out on him without even a goodbye, after spending the night with him, tell him that she didn't want to see him again—ever? Obviously not, if his presence here was anything to go by...

He was standing in front of the window looking out at the winter garden when she entered, slowly turning to look at her as he became aware of her presence.

Lilli's breath caught in her throat. God, he was handsome!

She hadn't really registered that last night, but in the clear light of day he was incredibly attractive, ruggedly so, his hair so dark a brown it almost appeared black, with those distinguished wings of silver at his temples. His skin was lightly tanned, features so finely hewn they might have been carved from stone, his eyes a light, enigmatic grey.

He was dressed very similarly to her, except he wore a fine checked jacket over his black jumper. Which meant he had been back to Geraldine's house this morning—if only to change his clothes!

He moved forward in long, easy movements, looking her critically up and down. 'Well, well, well,' he finally drawled. 'If it isn't Just Lilli—alias Elizabeth Bennett.' His voice hardened over the latter.

'Mr Devlin.' She nodded coolly in acknowledgement, none of her inner turmoil—she hoped!—in evidence.

She had chosen to go with this man the evening before for two reasons: to hurt her father, and hit out at Geraldine Simms. And at this moment Patrick Devlin seemed very much aware of that!

His mouth twisted mockingly. 'Mr. Devlin...? Really, Lilli, it's a little late for formality between us, isn't it?' he taunted.

She moved pointedly away from him; his derisive

manner was deliberately insulting. 'Why are you here?' She looked at him across the room with cool green eyes.

Dark brows rose at her tone. 'Well, I could say you left your bra behind and I've come to return it, but as you weren't wearing a bra last night...!'

'That's enough!' she snapped, two bright spots of embarrassed colour in her cheeks now.

'More than enough, I would say,' he agreed, his eyes glittering icily. 'Lilli, exactly what did you hope to achieve by going to bed with me?'

To hit out at her father, to hurt Geraldine Simms. Nothing more. But certainly nothing less. At the time she hadn't realised the man she had chosen to help her was actually the other woman's brother. She accepted it complicated things a little. Especially as he had come here today...

She deliberately gave a careless shrug. 'A good time.' It was half a question—because she couldn't remember whether or not they'd had a good time together!

He gave an acknowledging nod at her reply. 'And did you? Have a good time,' he persisted dryly at her puzzled expression.

She frowned. 'Didn't you?' she instantly returned. Two could play at this game!

His mouth quirked. 'Marks out of ten? Or do you have some other method of rating your lovers—?'

'There's no need to be insulting!' Lilli told him sharply.

'There's every need, damn you!' Patrick advanced towards her, his hand on her arm, fingers warm against her skin.

'Don't touch me!' she told him angrily, pulling away, and only succeeding in hurting herself. 'Let me go,' she ordered with every ounce of Bennett arrogance she possessed. This was her home, damn it, and he couldn't just come in here—uninvited!—and insult and manhandle her!

He thrust her away from him. 'I ought to break that beautiful neck of yours!' he ground out fiercely, eyes narrowed. 'You looked older last night... Exactly how old are you?' he bit out, his gaze sweeping over her scathingly.

She looked startled. 'What does my age have to do with anything?'

'Just answer the question, Lilli,' he rasped. 'And while you're at it explain to me exactly how the haughty Elizabeth Bennett ended up with a name like Lilli!'

Her own cheeks were flushed with anger now. 'Neither of those things is any of your business!'

'I'm making them so,' he told her levelly.

This man might be as good-looking as the devil, but he had the arrogance to match! Why hadn't she realised any of this the previous evening when she had met him? Because she hadn't been thinking straight, she acknowledged heavily, had been blinded by the fury she felt towards her father and the woman he was obviously involved with. This man's sister... She still had trouble connecting the two—they looked absolutely nothing alike!

'Well?' he prompted at her continued silence.

She glared at him resentfully, wanting him to leave but knowing he had no intention of doing so until he was good and ready—and he wasn't either of those things yet! 'I'm twenty-one,' she told him tautly.

'And?' He looked at her hardly.

'And three months,' she supplied challengingly, knowing it wasn't what he had been asking. But she had no intention of telling him that she had acquired the name Lilli because the baby brother she had adored, the baby brother who had died when he was only two years old, hadn't been able to manage the name Elizabeth. Just as she had no intention of telling him that she knew to the day exactly how old she was, because her mother, the mother she had also adored, had died on her twenty-first birthday... It was also the day her fiancée, her father's assistant, had walked out of her life...

He grimaced ruefully at her evasion. 'A mere child,' he ground out disgustedly. 'The sacrificial lamb!' He shook his head. 'I hate to tell you this, Lilli, but your efforts—enjoyable as they were!—were completely wasted.' His gaze hardened. 'If my own sister's pleadings failed to move me, you can be assured that a night of pleasure in your arms would have had even less effect!'

Lilli looked at him with haughty disdain. 'I don't have the least idea what you're talking about,' she snapped.

'No?' he queried sceptically.

'No,' she echoed tartly. 'I don't even know what you're doing here today. We were at a party, we decided to spend the night together—and that should have been the end of it. You came here, I didn't come to you,' she reminded him coldly.

'Actually, Lilli,' he drawled softly, 'I came to see your father, not you.'

Her head went back in astonishment. 'My father...?' she repeated in a puzzled voice.

Patrick nodded abruptly. 'Unfortunately, I was informed he isn't in,' he said grimly.

'So you asked to see me instead?' she realised incredulously.

'Correct,' he affirmed, with a slight inclination of his head. 'Sorry to disappoint you, Lilli,' he added.

She swallowed hard, quickly reassessing the situation. 'And just why did you want to see my father?'

Patrick looked at her with narrowed eyes. 'I'm sure you already know the answer to that question.'

'Because he's having a relationship with your sister?' Lilli scorned. 'It must keep you very busy if you pay personal calls on all her lovers in this way!'

Anger flared briefly in the grey depths of his eyes, and then they became glacially enigmatic, that gaze sweeping over her with deliberate assessment. 'I'm sure you keep your father just as busy,' he drawled.

After her comment about Geraldine, she had probably deserved that remark. Unfortunately, both this man and his sister brought out the worst in her; she wasn't usually a bitchy person. But then, this whole situation was unusual!

'Perhaps he's paying a similar call on you at this very moment?' Lilli returned.

'I very much doubt it.' Patrick gave a smile. 'It hasn't been my impression, so far in our acquaintance, that your father has ever deliberately gone out of his way to meet me!'

Her eyes widened. 'The two of you have met?' If they had, her father hadn't mentioned that particular fact earlier!

'Several times,' Patrick confirmed enigmatically.

Exactly how long had her father been involved with Geraldine? Lilli had assumed it was a very recent thing, but if the two men had met 'several times'...

'Perhaps you could pass on a message to him that we will be meeting again, too. Very soon,' Patrick added grimly, walking to the door.

Lilli watched him frowningly. 'You're leaving...?' She hadn't meant her voice to sound wistful at all—and yet somehow it did. In the fifteen minutes Patrick had been here he had made insulting comments to her, enigmatic remarks about her father—but he hadn't really said anything. She wasn't really sure what she had expected him to say... But the two of them had spent the night together, and—

He turned at the door, dark brows raised questioningly. 'Do we have anything else to say to each other?' he questioned in a bored voice.

No, of course they didn't. They had had nothing to say to each other from the beginning. It was just that—

'Ten, Lilli,' he drawled softly. 'You were a ten,' he explained dryly as she gave him a puzzled look.

He laughed huskily as his meaning became clear and her cheeks suffused with heated colour.

She hadn't wanted to know—hadn't asked—

'I'll let myself out, Lilli,' he volunteered, and did so, the door closing softly behind him.

Which was just as well—because Lilli had been rooted to the spot after that last statement.

Ten...

And she didn't remember a single moment of it...

CHAPTER THREE

'I WANT to know exactly what is going on, Daddy,' Lilli told him firmly, having waited in the sitting-room for two hours before he came home, fortified by the tray of tea things Emily had brought in to her. After Patrick Devlin's departure, Lilli had felt in need of something, and whisky, at that hour of the day, had been out of the question. Although the man was enough to drive anyone to drink!

She had heard her father enter the house, accosting him in the hallway as he walked towards the wide stair-case.

He turned at the sound of her voice, his expression grim. 'I was left in no doubt by you earlier that you didn't want to hear anything more about Geraldine.'

'I still don't,' Lilli told him impatiently. 'Her brother, however, is a different matter!'

'Patrick?' her father replied.

Her mouth twisted. 'Unless she has another brother— yes!'

Her father stiffened, striding forcefully across the hall-way to join her as she went into the sitting-room, closing the door firmly behind him. 'What about him?' he said warily.

She gave an impatient sigh. 'That's what I just asked you!'

'You spent the night with him, Lilli,' her father re-minded her. 'I would have thought you would know all there is to know about the man! We none of us have defences in bed. Or so I'm told…'

She bit back the reply she would have liked to make; that sort of conversation would take them absolutely nowhere, as it had this morning. 'I'm not talking about the man's prowess—or otherwise!—in the bedroom,' she snapped. 'He said the two of you know each other.'

'Did he?' her father returned with studied indifference.

'Daddy!' She glared at her father's back as he stood looking out of the window now—very much as Patrick had done earlier. He was trying to give the impression that the subject of the other man bored him, and yet, somehow, she knew that it didn't…

He sighed. 'I'm sorry. I just didn't realise the two of you had spent part of your night together discussing me—'

'We didn't,' Lilli cut in. 'He was here earlier.'

Her father froze, slowly turning to face her. 'Devlin came here?'

She wasn't wrong; she was sure she wasn't; she had never seen this emotion in her father before, but he actually looked slightly fearful. And it had something to do with Patrick Devlin…

'Yes, he was here,' she confirmed steadily. 'And he said some things—'

'He had no right, damn him!' her father told her fiercely, his hands clenched into fists at his sides.

'I'm your daughter—'

'And this is a business matter,' he barked tensely. 'If I had wanted to tell you about it then I would have done so.'

'Tell me now?' Lilli encouraged softly. Her father had mentioned this morning that Patrick Devlin was the chairman of Paradise Bank—could that have something to do with this 'business matter'? Although, as far as she was aware, her family had always banked with Cleveley…

'I told you, Patrick Devlin *is* Paradise Bank,' her father grated.

And she was none the wiser for his repeating the fact! 'Yes?'

'Don't you ever read the newspapers, Lilli?' her father said tersely. 'Or are you more like your mother than I realised, and only interested in what Bennett International Hotels can give you in terms of money and lifestyle?'

The accusation hung between them, everything suddenly seeming very quiet; even the air was still.

Lilli stared at her father, barely breathing, a tight pain in her chest.

Her father stared back at her, obviously mortified at what he had just said, his face very pale.

They never talked about her mother, or baby Robbie; they had, by tacit agreement, never talked about the loss of either.

Lilli drew in a deep breath. 'I know Mummy had her faults—'

'I'm sorry, Lilli—'

They had both begun talking at the same time, both coming to an abrupt halt, once again staring at each other, awkwardly this time. The last three months had been difficult; Lilli's grief at her mother's death was something she hadn't been able to share with anyone. Not even her father.

She had known that her father had his own pain to deal with. The years during which her mother's illness had deteriorated had been even more difficult for him

than they had for Lilli, her mother's moods fluctuating
between self-pity and anger. It had been hard to cope
with, Lilli freely acknowledged. But she had had no idea
how bitter her father had become...

'I shouldn't have said that.' Her father ran a weary
hand through dark hair liberally peppered with grey.
'I'm sorry, Lilli.'

She wasn't sure whether he was apologising for the
remarks about her mother, or for the fact that he felt the
way he did...

'No, you shouldn't,' she agreed quietly. 'But a lot of
things have been said and done in the last twenty-four
hours that shouldn't have been.' She included her own
behaviour with Patrick Devlin in that! 'Perhaps it would
be better if we just forgot about them?' She certainly
wanted to forget last night!

'I wish we could, Lilli.' Her father sat down heavily
in one of the armchairs, shaking his head. 'But I don't
think Devlin will let either of us do that.' He leant his
head back against the chair, his eyes closed. 'What did
he have to say when he came here earlier?' He opened
his eyes to look at her frowningly.

Besides marking her as a ten...?

'Not a lot, Daddy.' She crossed the room to kneel on
the carpet at his feet. 'Although he did say to tell you
the two of you would be meeting again. Soon. Tell me
what's going on, Daddy?' She looked up at him ap-
pealingly.

He reached out to smooth gently the loose tendrils of
dark hair away from her cheeks. 'You're so young,
Lilli.' He sounded pained. 'So very young,' he groaned.
'You give the outward impression of being so cool and
self-possessed, and yet...'

'It's just an impression,' she acknowledged ruefully.

'How well you know me, Daddy.' She gave a wistful smile.

'I should do,' he said with gentle affection. 'I love you very much, Lilli. No matter what happens, I hope you never forget that.' He gave a heavy sigh.

Lilli once again felt that chill of foreboding down her spine. What was going to happen? And what did Patrick Devlin have to do with it? Because she didn't doubt that he was at the root of her father's problem.

Her father straightened determinedly in his chair, that air of defeat instantly dispelled. 'Devlin and I are involved in some business that isn't going quite the way he wishes it would,' he explained briskly.

Lilli frowned, realising that, with this blunt statement, her father had decided not to tell her anything. 'He called me a sacrificial lamb,' she persisted.

'Did he, indeed?' her father rapped out harshly. 'What the hell does he think I am?' he cried angrily, rising forcefully to his feet. 'Devlin is right, Lilli—it's past time the two of us met again. Damn Gerry and her diplomatic approach—'

'About Geraldine Simms—'

'She's not for discussion, Lilli,' her father cut in defensively, those few minutes of father-daughter closeness definitely over.

Obviously Geraldine Simms was too important in his life to be discussed with her! It made Lilli question exactly how long this relationship with the other woman had been going on. Since her mother's death—or before that? The thought of her father having an affair with a woman like Geraldine Simms while her mother was still alive made Lilli feel ill. He couldn't have—could he...?

Lilli stood up too, eyes flashing deeply emerald. 'In

that case,' she rebutted angrily, 'neither is the night I spent with her brother!'

'Lilli!' Her father stopped her as she was about to storm out of the room.

She turned slowly. 'Yes?' she said curtly.

'Stay away from Devlin,' he advised heavily. 'He's trouble.'

He might be, and until a short time ago she had been only too happy with the idea of never setting eyes on him again. But not any more. Patrick Devlin was the other half of this puzzle, and if her father wouldn't tell her what was going on perhaps Patrick would!

She met her father's gaze unblinkingly. 'Stay away from Geraldine Simms,' she mocked. 'She's trouble.'

Her father steadily met her rebellious gaze for several long seconds, and then he wearily shook his head. 'This is so much deeper than you can possibly realise. You're playing with fire where Devlin is concerned. He's a barracuda in a city suit,' he added bitterly.

'Sounds like a fascinating combination,' Lilli replied.

'More like deadly,' her father rasped, scowling darkly. 'Lilli, I'm ordering you to stay away from him!'

Her eyes widened in shock. This was much more serious than she had even imagined; she couldn't remember the last time her father had ordered her to do anything. If he ever had. But the fact that he did it now only made her all the more determined.

The real problem with that was she had no idea—yet!—how to even make contact with Patrick Devlin again, without it seeming as if she was doing exactly that. Because she had a feeling he would react exactly as her father was doing if she went to him and asked for answers to her questions: refuse to give any!

Well, she might be young, as both men had already

stated quite clearly today, but she was the daughter of one man, and had spent the previous night in the arms of the other—she certainly wasn't a child, and she wasn't about to be treated like one. By either of them!

'Save that tone of voice for your employees, Father,' she told him coldly. 'Of which I—thankfully!—am not one!' She closed the door decisively behind her as she left the room.

It was only once she was safely outside in the hallway that she allowed some of her defiance to leave her. But she had meant every word she'd said in there, she would get to the bottom of this mystery. And she knew the very person to help her do that...

'Sally!' she said warmly a few minutes later when the other woman answered her call after the tenth ring. She had begun to think Sally must be out. And that didn't fit in with her plans at all. 'It's Lilli.'

'Wow, that was quick,' Sally returned lightly. 'I didn't expect to hear from you again for weeks.'

Lilli forced a bright laugh. 'I said I would call you,' she reminded her.

'It's a little late in the day for lunch,' Sally said dryly. 'Although to be honest,' she added confidingly, 'I've only just got out of bed. That was some party last night!'

Lilli wouldn't know. 'Any luck with that gorgeous man?' she said playfully—knowing full well there hadn't been; her father had spent the night with Geraldine Simms.

'None at all.' Sally sounded disappointed. 'But then, with Gerry on the hunt, I never expected it. She monopolised the man all night, and then—'

'Are you free for dinner this evening?' Lilli cut in sharply—she knew what came 'then'!

'Well...I was due to go to the Jameses' party this

evening, but it will just be like every other party I've been to this month. Christmas-time is a bitch, isn't it? Everyone and his cousin throws a party—and invites exactly the same people to every one! In all honesty, I'm all partied out. And there's another ten days to go yet!' Sally groaned with feeling.

'Does that mean you're free for dinner?' Lilli prompted.

'Name the place!' The grin could be heard in Sally's voice.

Lilli did, choosing one of her own favourite restaurants, knowing the other woman would like it too. She also promised that it was her treat; Sally knew 'everyone and his cousin', and anything there was to know about them. Lilli didn't doubt she would know about Patrick Devlin too...

She wasn't disappointed in her choice of informant!

'Patrick!' Even the way Sally said his name spoke volumes. 'Now there *is* a gorgeous man. Tall, dark, handsome— He's Gerry's brother, you know—'

'I do know,' Lilli confirmed—she knew now!

'He's also intelligent, rich—oh yes, very rich.' Sally laughed softly.

'And single.' It was almost a question—because Lilli wasn't absolutely sure of his marital status. She had been to bed with the man, and she didn't even know whether he was married!

'He is now,' Sally nodded, nibbling on one of the prawns she had chosen to start her meal. 'Sanchia wasn't the faithful kind, and so he went through rather a messy divorce about five years ago. Sanchia took him for millions. Personally, I would rather have kept the man, but

Sanchia settled for the cash and moved back to France, where she originally came from.'

Sanchia... Patrick had been married to a woman called Sanchia. A woman who had been unfaithful to him. She couldn't have known him very well if she had thought he would put up with that; Lilli had only known him twenty-four hours, but, even so, she knew he was a man who kept what he had. Exclusively.

But at least he wasn't married now, which was a relief to hear after last night. Although there was still so much Lilli wanted to know about him...

'What does he do?' Lilli frowned; chairman of a bank didn't tell her anything.

'I just told you.' Sally laughed. 'He makes millions.'

'And then gives them away to ex-wives,' Lilli scorned; that didn't sound very intelligent to her!

'One ex-wife,' Sally corrected her. 'And he didn't give it away. It was probably worth it to him to get that embarrassment out of his life. Sanchia liked men, and made no secret of the fact...'

'She sounds a lot like his sister,' Lilli said bitterly. How could her father have been so stupid as to have got mixed up with such a family?

'Gerry's okay,' Sally said grudgingly. 'Although Patrick is even better,' she added suggestively.

Lilli gave her a guarded look. 'Sally, you haven't— You and he haven't—'

'I should be so lucky!' Sally laughed again ruefully. 'But Patrick doesn't. Not any more. Not since Sanchia,' she amended wistfully.

Lilli hoped she succeeded in hiding the shock she felt at this last statement. Because Patrick most certainly did! At least, he had last night. With her...

Sally gave her a considering look. 'You do realise I'm

going to have a few questions of my own at the end of this conversation?' she teased. 'And the first one is going to be, just when and where did you get to meet Patrick? As far as I'm aware, he's lived in New York for the last five years, and he's very rarely seen over here.'

Lilli kept her expression deliberately bland. 'Hey, I'm the one buying you dinner, remember,' she reminded her. She liked Sally very much, found her great fun to go out with, but she was also aware that her friend was the biggest gossip in London—that was the reason she had been the perfect choice for this conversation in the first place! 'Besides, just what makes you think I have met him?' She opened widely innocent eyes.

Sally gave a throaty chuckle, attracting the attention of several of the men at adjoining tables. Not that she seemed in the least concerned by this male interest; she was still looking thoughtfully at Lilli. 'Only a woman who had actually met Patrick would show this much interest in him; he's a presence to be reckoned with!'

Well, from all accounts—his account!—Lilli had met that challenge all too capably. 'I'm more interested in the business side of his life than his personal one.' Now that she had assured herself he wasn't married or seriously involved with anyone!

Sally shrugged. 'I've just told you he's based in New York. Chairman of Paradise Bank. Rich as Croesus. What else is there to know?'

His business connection to her father! 'English business interests?' she prompted skilfully.

'Oh, that one's easy,' the other woman returned. 'It was all in the newspapers a couple of months ago.' She smiled warmly at the waiter as he brought their main course.

Lilli barely stopped herself grinding her teeth together

in frustration. What had been in the newspapers months ago? 'I was a little out of touch with things at the time,' she reminded Sally once they were alone again.

'I'm sorry, of course you were.' Sally at once looked contrite. 'Paradise Bank took over Cleveley Bank.'

Cleveley Bank... Her father's bank. But that still didn't make a lot of sense to Lilli. Bennett International Hotels had shown a profit since before she was born, so it couldn't possibly have anything to do with them.

'Personally, I thought it was wonderful news.' Sally grinned across at Lilli as she gave her a puzzled glance. 'It means Patrick will probably start spending more time in England. More chance for us eager women to make a play at being the second Mrs Patrick Devlin,' she explained. 'I could quite easily give up this round of parties and the bachelor-girl life if I had Patrick coming home to me every evening!'

'It wasn't enough for the first Mrs Devlin,' Lilli said sharply as she realised she was actually jealous of Sally's undoubted interest in Patrick. Ridiculous! The man was arrogant, insulting, dangerous. And she had spent last night in his arms...

'Sanchia was stupid,' Sally rejoined unhesitatingly. 'She thought Patrick was so besotted with her that he would forgive her little indiscretions with other men.' Sally shook her head disgustedly. 'What Patrick owns, he owns exclusively.'

Exactly what Lilli had thought earlier! 'Not even Patrick Devlin can own people,' she said quickly.

'You have met him!' Sally said speculatively.

She could feel the guilty colour in her cheeks. 'Perhaps,' she acknowledged grudgingly. Obviously Patrick hadn't spent any time at the party last night, otherwise Sally would have seen him there too...

'But you're not telling, hmm?' Sally said knowingly. 'Oh, don't worry, Lilli.' She lightly touched Lilli's arm. 'I wouldn't be telling anyone about it either if I had Patrick tucked away in my pocket. But you will invite me to the wedding, won't you?'

Lilli drew back in shocked revulsion at the very suggestion. 'I think you've misunderstood my interest, Sally—'

'Not in the least.' The other woman gave her a conspiratorial wink. 'And if you have him, Lilli, hang onto him. There are dozens of women out there—including me!—who would snap him up given the chance!'

'But—'

'I won't tell a soul, Lilli,' Sally assured her softly. 'It will be our little secret.'

Perhaps her choice of informant hadn't been such a wise one, after all. Lilli had forgotten, in her need to know more about Patrick Devlin, just how much Sally loved what she considered a tasty piece of gossip—and how she loved sharing it with other people, despite what she might have just said to the contrary! The news of Lilli's interest in Patrick Devlin would be all over London by tomorrow if she didn't think of some way to avert it!

Her only hope seemed to be to give the other woman such a good time she wouldn't remember where they had spent the evening, let alone what they had talked about at the beginning of it—least of all Patrick Devlin.

A bottle of champagne later and Lilli wasn't sure what they had talked about either! Sally's suggestion that they go on to a club seemed an excellent idea. The restaurant staff seemed quite happy to see their last customers leave too, ordering a taxi to take them on to the club.

'I know I'm going to regret this some time tomorrow

when I finally wake up,' Sally giggled as they got out
of the taxi outside the club. 'But what the hell!'

Lilli's sentiments exactly. It seemed like years, not
just months, since she had been out and enjoyed herself
like this. Last night certainly didn't count!

She was enjoying herself, couldn't remember when
she had had so much fun, dancing, chatting with friends
she hadn't seen for such a long time, once again the life
and soul of the party, as she always used to be.

'Well, if it isn't Just Lilli, come out to play once
again,' drawled an all-too-familiar voice close behind
her. 'It's our dance, I believe,' Patrick Devlin added
forcefully—and before Lilli could so much as utter a
protest she found herself on the dance floor with him.

And it wasn't one of the fast numbers she had danced
to earlier, the evening was now mellowing out into early
morning, and so was the music. Lilli found herself firmly
moulded against Patrick's chest and thighs, his arms
about her waist not ungentle, but unyielding nonetheless.

And Lilli knew, because she tried to move, pulling
back to look up at him with furious green eyes. 'Let me
go,' she ordered between gritted teeth.

God knew what Sally was going to make of this after
their earlier conversation! Not that Lilli could be in the
least responsible for this meeting; she hadn't even realised he was at the club, certainly hadn't seen him
amongst the crowd of people here. But he had obviously
seen her!

For all that she was tall herself, the high heels on her
shoes making her even more so, she still had to tilt her
head to look up into his face. 'I said—'

'I heard you,' he returned unconcernedly, continuing
to move slowly in rhythm to the music, his warm breath
stirring the loose tendrils of hair at her temples.

She glared up at him. 'I thought you didn't like parties,' she said accusingly. He had no right being here, spoiling her evening once again.

He glanced down at her. 'This isn't a party,' he dismissed easily. 'But you're right—I don't particularly like noisy clubs like this one. I came here to conclude a business deal.'

Business! She should have known he had a calculated reason for being here. 'Like last night,' she said waspishly.

His mouth tightened. 'Last night I expected a quiet dinner party with my sister, with perhaps a dozen or so other guests. Not including your father,' he bit out tersely. 'Or that madhouse I walked into—and as quickly walked out of again! To the kitchen, as it happens. Which was where I met you.'

Lilli stiffened in his arms. 'Earlier today you seemed to have the impression that *I* had deliberately found *you*,' she reminded him.

He shrugged unconcernedly. 'Earlier today I was talking to the haughty Elizabeth Bennett. Tonight you're Just Lilli again.' He looked down at her admiringly. 'I like your hair loose like this.' He ran one of his hands through her long, silky black tresses. 'And as for this dress…!' His eyes darkened in colour as he looked down at the figure-hugging black dress.

All Lilli could think of at that moment was that they were attracting too much attention. Obviously Patrick was well known by quite a lot of the people here, and the speculation in the room about the two of them was tangible. Especially as Sally was in the midst of one particular crowd, chatting away feverishly, Lilli sure their 'little secret' was no longer any such thing!

'I wouldn't worry about them if I were you,' Patrick

followed her gaze—and, it seemed, her dismayed thoughts. 'Gossip, true or false, is what keeps most of them going. It's probably because they lead such boring lives themselves,' he added scornfully.

She knew he was right; it was one of the aspects of being part of a 'crowd' that she hadn't liked. But, even so, she wasn't sure she particularly liked being the subject—along with Patrick Devlin—of that gossip, either.

Patrick made no effort to leave the dance floor as one song ended and another began, continuing to guide her smoothly around. 'Forget about them, Lilli,' he suggested as she still frowned.

She would have liked to, but unfortunately she had a feeling that by tomorrow half of London would believe she was involved in an affair with Patrick Devlin. And the other half wouldn't give a damn whom she was involved with—because they had never heard of her or Patrick!

'Lilli and Elizabeth Bennett are one and the same person.' She coldly answered his earlier remark.

'No, they aren't. Just Lilli is warm and giving, fun to be with. Elizabeth Bennett is as cold as ice.' He looked down at her with mocking grey eyes. 'I'm curious; which one were you with your ex-fiancé?'

How did he—? Not a single person she had met this evening had so much as mentioned Andy, let alone their broken engagement. Surely Patrick hadn't done the same as her—spent part of the day finding out more about her…?

If so, *why* had he?

'Don't bother to answer that, Lilli; I think I can guess.' Patrick grinned. 'If you had been Just Lilli with him then he would probably still be around—despite his other interests.'

Lilli deeply resented his even talking about her broken engagement. She had been deeply distressed by her mother's death, and then for Andy to walk out on her too...! It had seemed like a nightmare at the time.

She had just started to feel she was coming out of it when she had been plunged into another one—with the name of Patrick Devlin!

'Just Lilli is a pretty potent woman, you know.' Patrick's arms tightened about her as he moulded her even closer against his body, showing her all too forcibly just how 'potent' he found her! 'In fact, I haven't been able to get her out of my mind all day.'

She swallowed hard, not immune herself to the intimacy of the situation, her nipples firm and tingling, her thighs aching warmly. 'And Elizabeth Bennett?' she prompted huskily.

'A spoilt little rich girl who needs her bottom spanked,' he replied unhesitatingly.

Lilli gasped. How dared he—? Just who did he think he was, suddenly appearing in her life, and then proceeding to arrogantly—?

'And if I had been her fiancé that's exactly what I would have done,' he continued unconcernedly.

They were still dancing slowly to the music, the room still as noisy and crowded, and yet at the moment they could have been the only two people in the room, their gazes locked in silent battle, grey eyes calmly challenging, green eyes spitting fire.

Finally Lilli was the one to break that deadlock as she pulled away from him, ending the dance abruptly, the two of them simply standing on the dance floor now. 'I would never have agreed to marry you in the first place,' she told him insultingly.

Patrick shrugged, totally unmoved by her anger. 'But you will, Lilli,' he said softly. 'I guarantee that you will.'

'I—you— Never!' She spluttered her indignation. 'You're mad!' She shook her head incredulously.

'But not, thank God, about you,' he said calmly. 'I've been there, and done that. And I've realised that loving the person you marry is a recipe for disaster. I've found qualities in you that are infinitely more preferable.'

'Such as?' she challenged. She still couldn't believe they were having this conversation!

'Loyalty, for one. A true sense of family.' He shrugged. 'And, of course, I find you very desirable.' This last was added, it seemed, as an afterthought.

Loyalty? A sense of family! Desire! They weren't reasons for marrying someone—

She was *not* going to marry Patrick Devlin!

He was mad. Completely. Utterly insane!

His mouth quirked with amusement as he saw those emotions flashing across her expressive face. 'A month, Lilli,' he told her softly. 'You will be my wife within the month.'

Lilli looked up at him frowningly; his gaze was enigmatic now. He sounded so sure of himself, so calmly certain...

She was not going to marry him.

She was not!

CHAPTER FOUR

'HE WHAT?' her father gasped as he once again sat across the breakfast table from her.

Lilli sighed, still slightly shell-shocked about last night herself. She had walked away from Patrick, and the club, after his ridiculous claim, still had trouble even now believing he could possibly have said what he did. But the bouquet of red roses, delivered early this morning, told her that Patrick had indeed stated last night that he intended marrying her.

Her father had been intrigued by the delivery of the roses when he'd joined her for breakfast, especially since there was no accompanying card with the flowers to say who they were from. But Lilli had no doubts who had sent them; only someone as arrogant as Patrick Devlin could have red roses delivered before the shops were even open!

'Your business associate, Mr Devlin, has decided he wants to marry me,' she repeated wearily, pushing her scrambled eggs distractedly about her plate. She couldn't possibly eat anything after the delivery of the roses!

Her father had lost interest in his bacon and eggs too now. 'What the hell did you do to him the other night?'

Lilli could feel the blush in her cheeks. She couldn't remember being with Patrick Devlin the night before last; she only wished she could. Well...part of her wished she could. The other part of her just wished it had never happened at all. Because Patrick wasn't going to let her forget it, that was for sure!

'I don't think his marriage proposal has anything to do with that,' she dismissed hurriedly.

Or did it? After all, he *had* said she was a ten...

Her father looked at her through narrowed lids. 'What does it have to do with, then?'

Lilli met his gaze steadily. 'You tell me?' She arched questioning brows.

'I have no idea.' Her father stood up, obviously having trouble coming to terms with this strange turn of events. *He* was having trouble coming to terms with it? *She* found it totally incredible.

'Why ever does he want to marry you?' Her father scowled darkly.

'Having already "had" me?' Lilli returned dryly.

'I didn't mean that at all!' Her father looked flustered. Dressed in a dark suit and formal tie and shirt, he was on his way to his office. Although he seemed in no hurry to get there... 'The two of you barely know— The two of you only met two days ago,' he hastily corrected as Lilli's expression clearly questioned his initial choice of words.

'Oh, don't imagine this proposal is based on love,' Lilli assured him. '"Loyalty" and "desire" were the words Patrick used.'

'Loyalty and—! Do you have "loyalty" and "desire" for him?' her father said incredulously.

She didn't even know the man!

Patrick Devlin was obviously a successful businessman, so she supposed he was to be admired for that, but whether or not he was an honest one was another matter. If her father's state of anxiety at being involved in business with him was anything to go by, then he probably wasn't.

As for desire... She supposed she must have wanted him the other night...

If she were honest, she had felt a stirring of that attraction towards him last night as well—

'The whole thing is ridiculous!' She stood up abruptly too. 'The man has obviously tried marrying for love, and it was not a success, so now he seems to have decided to marry for totally different reasons.' Loyalty and desire...

Her father shook his head. 'Why does he want to marry at all?'

'It's time I provided the Devlin name with a couple of heirs,' drawled that all-too-familiar voice. The two of them turned to confront Patrick Devlin, a flustered Emily standing in the doorway behind him.

'I did ask Mr Devlin to wait, but—'

'Who knows?' Patrick continued softly. 'After the other night, perhaps Lilli is already pregnant with my child.'

Lilli gasped, her father went pale—and poor Emily looked as if she was about to faint!

Which wasn't surprising, in the circumstances. How dared Patrick Devlin just walk in here as if he owned the place? And make such outrageous remarks too!

Lilli turned dismissively to the young maid. 'That will be all, thank you, Emily.' She had no intention of giving the young girl any more information for gossip among the household staff.

'Perhaps you could bring us all a fresh pot of coffee?' Patrick Devlin smiled disarmingly at Emily before she could make good her escape. 'I'm sure we could all do with some,' he added dryly as he sat down—uninvited— at the dining-table.

Emily hesitated in the doorway, looking uncertainly

at Lilli. Patrick Devlin might be behaving as if he owned the place, but Emily, at least, knew that he didn't!

'A pot of coffee will be fine, Emily,' Lilli said, waiting for the maid to leave and close the door behind her before turning to Patrick Devlin. 'What are you doing here?' she demanded, this man, with his arrogant behaviour, didn't deserve customary politeness!

He met her question unconcernedly. 'Waiting for fresh coffee to arrive,' he replied easily. 'Good morning, Richard. Has Lilli told you our good news?'

'If you're referring to that ridiculous marriage proposal,' her father blustered, 'then—'

'It isn't ridiculous, Richard,' Patrick cut in steadily. 'Ah, I see the roses arrived,' he said with satisfaction. 'I hope you like red roses?' He smiled across at Lilli.

There probably wasn't a woman alive who didn't, especially if you happened to be the lucky woman who received them. But in this case it depended who the sender was!

'You can't marry Lilli,' her father told the other man fiercely.

'Why not?' Patrick returned lightly. 'She isn't married already, is she?'

'No, of course not,' her father denied impatiently. 'But you—'

'I'm not married, either,' Patrick told him firmly. 'In which case, I can see no obstacle to our marrying each other.'

'But you don't know each other—'

'I know Lilli is beautiful. Popular—if last night is anything to go by. Well educated. And, as your daughter, an accomplished hostess. There's no doubting she's young, and she certainly seems healthy enough—'

'To provide you with those Devlin heirs you mentioned?' Lilli broke in disgustedly. 'You sound as if you're discussing buying a horse, or—or arranging a business contract, not considering taking a wife!'

'Marriage is a business, Lilli,' Patrick told her evenly, eyes coldly unmoving. 'And anyone who approaches it from any other angle is just asking for trouble. Not that it will be all business, of course,' he continued smoothly. 'I'm well aware of the fact that women like a little romance attached to things. I'm quite willing to play my role in that department too. If you think it necessary.' His derisive expression was indicative of his own feelings on the subject.

'Hence the sending of the roses,' Lilli guessed scornfully.

'Hence the roses.' He nodded in acknowledgement. 'Ah, coffee.' He turned to Emily as she came in carrying the steaming pot. 'Thank you.' He nodded to her, looking back at Lilli and her father once they were alone again. 'Shall I pour? Although you look as if you're on your way to your office, Richard, so perhaps you don't want another cup of coffee?' He quirked dark brows.

This man's arrogance was like nothing Lilli had ever encountered before; he had already taken over the staff, and now he appeared to be telling her father what to do too!

'Sit down and have some coffee, Daddy.' Lilli looked at Patrick pointedly as she resumed her own seat at the table—on the opposite side to him. 'I'm sure Patrick won't be staying very long.' She looked challengingly at the younger man.

'Oh, I'm in no hurry to leave,' Patrick replied, completely unperturbed by the fact that he obviously wasn't welcome here. 'I have nothing to do today until my business appointment with you this afternoon, Richard.' He

looked across at the older man. 'You did ask my secretary for a three o'clock appointment, didn't you?' he
queried pleasantly, pouring the three cups of coffee as
he spoke.

Her father sat down abruptly. 'I did,' he confirmed
gruffly.

'Good.' Patrick grinned his satisfaction. 'That means
I'll have time to take Lilli to lunch first.'

'I—'

'You have to eat, Lilli.' Patrick gently forestalled her
refusal.

'Not with you, I don't,' she told him heatedly; he
wasn't being polite, so why should she be?

'What do you think, Richard?' He looked at Lilli's
father. 'Don't you think Lilli would enjoy having lunch
with me?'

Richard Bennett looked frustrated once again. 'I—'

'As my father won't be the one having lunch with
you, his opinion on the subject is irrelevant!' Lilli
snapped frostily.

Patrick raised dark brows at her vehemence. 'There
speaks Miss Bennett,' he drawled, his expression innocent.

Too damned innocent! Lilli remembered all too well
what his opinion of Elizabeth Bennett was!

'Mm, this is good coffee,' Patrick said appreciatively
as he sipped the hot brew. 'I think I must have drunk
too much champagne last night,' he opined ruefully.

Lilli glared at him. 'Is that your excuse for your outrageous announcement last night?' she said contemptuously.

'Do I take it you're referring to my marriage proposal?' He frowned.

'Of course.'

'Sorry for the confusion, but I don't consider it an "outrageous announcement",' he returned. 'Especially as I've made it again this morning. Several times,' he added in a bored voice.

'And I have dismissed it as ludicrous—several times!' Lilli told him with feeling.

'You know, Richard...' Patrick looked calmly across the table. 'You really should have taken Lilli in hand years ago—you've made the job of becoming her husband all the more difficult by not doing so!'

Lilli was so enraged by this last casually condemning remark about her independent nature that for a moment she couldn't even speak.

And her father laughed!

Considering he hadn't done so for some time, it was good to hear—but not at her expense! There was nothing in the least funny about this situation.

Her father looked a little shamefaced, sobering slowly. 'I'm sorry, Lilli.' He touched her hand in apology. 'It was just that—well—'

'He knows I'm right,' Patrick put in. 'Although I'm probably the first person brave enough to actually say as much.'

She had realised the first night she met him that he was very direct, but she hadn't known it was to the point of rudeness. What on earth had she been thinking of two nights ago, becoming involved with such a man? The trouble was, she hadn't been thinking at all, had just wanted to hit out and hurt, the way she had been hurt when she saw her father with Geraldine Simms.

How that had rebounded on her! Spending the night with Patrick had changed nothing—except that the man now seemed to think he was going to marry her! Oh, she had hurt her father, but he was still seeing Geraldine, and now she, it seemed, was stuck with the infuriating Patrick Devlin!

'Although I can quite easily see how it happened, Richard.' Patrick continued his conversation with her father. 'Lilli is the sort of woman you want to spoil.'

'Thank you.' Laughter still gleamed in her father's eyes. 'She was incredibly endearing as a little girl.'

'I can imagine.' Patrick nodded, turning back to Lilli. 'Make sure you stop me from spoiling our daughters, Lilli, because they're sure to look like you, and—'

'Daughters!' She gasped at the plural. 'How many children do you want?'

'You see, I knew you would come round.' Patrick grinned at her approvingly. 'I would like you to be mother to two sons and two daughters.'

Four children. 'You said "a couple of heirs" earlier,' she reminded him.

He shrugged. 'Four sounds a much better number. Besides, I'm sure you'll look even more beautiful when you're pregnant than you do now, so I'll—'

Her father stood up noisily, effectively cutting off the indignant reply he could see Lilli had been about to make. 'I'll leave the two of you to continue discussing this,' he said. 'And the outcome, as I've told you before—' he turned to Patrick with narrowed eyes '—will have no bearing whatsoever on our—business arrangement.'

'Agreed,' the other man conceded easily. 'Although, as your son-in-law, I could be more helpful to you…'

'I don't think so,' Lilli's father replied slowly, giving Lilli a considering look. 'As my son-in-law, you're likely to end up with a knife sticking in your back on your wedding night!'

Patrick's mouth twisted humorously. 'All the more

reason for you to encourage the marriage, I would have thought,' he drawled.

'Ah, but then I would have to explain to Gerry how I let this happen to the older brother she so obviously adores. And, as I know to my cost,' Richard dramatically added, 'an angry and upset Gerry is a force to be reckoned with!'

'But you have no personal objections to this marriage?' Patrick prompted.

'None at all—because it will never happen,' Lilli's father returned easily. 'I know my Lilli.' He kissed her lightly on the forehead in parting. 'I'll see you later, Devlin,' he said hardly before leaving the room.

Patrick turned back to Lilli with calm grey eyes. '*Does* he know you?' he asked. 'Did he really believe you could go off and spend the night with a man you had only just met?'

She could too easily recall the pained expression on her father's face yesterday morning. No, her father hadn't believed her capable of that. But then, neither had she!

Her head went back in haughty dismissal. 'No one has to spend a lifetime paying for the mistake of one night of stupidity any more.'

'Don't they?' Patrick said softly, standing up to move round the table to stand at her side. 'The other night wasn't stupid, Lilli,' he told her huskily as he pulled her easily to her feet to stand in front of him. 'I wouldn't still have it on my mind if it had been. You were warm and responsive, gave yourself—'

'Stop it!' she cut in desperately, not wanting to hear about what she couldn't even remember. Or did she...

Even as he spoke she had images flitting in and out of her head, of the two of them in bed together, of their bodies entwined, of Patrick's lips and hands on her body, of her own pleasure in those caresses—

No! She didn't want to remember. It had been a mistake, and not one for which she intended paying for the rest of her life.

'But you were, Lilli,' Patrick told her, suddenly very close. 'And you did.'

He was too close! She could smell his aftershave, see black specks amongst the grey in his irises, feel the warmth of his breath on her cheek, knew—

His mouth, as it claimed hers, was warm and gently caressing, his arms enfolding her against the hardness of his body, moulding her to each sinewed curve, deepening the kiss, desire and wanting suddenly taking over.

Lilli felt the same need, her body responding instinctively to the caress of his hands down her spine, shivers of delight coursing through her body, her mouth opening to the intimacy of his kiss, a feeling of hard possession sweeping over her.

It was the force of that feeling that made her at last struggle to be free of his arms. Yes, she responded to him. Yes, she could feel the heat in her body for him, for the need of him. But she didn't want to be possessed, by him or any other man. Especially not by Patrick Devlin!

Patrick felt her struggles and at once released her, his eyes dark with his own emotions as he looked at her. 'It would work between us, Lilli,' he whispered. 'What further proof do you want?'

Heated colour warmed her cheeks. 'Physically we—'

'Match completely,' he completed for her.

Lilli looked at him. 'We have a certain response to each other,' she allowed. 'But when you came here yesterday afternoon you believed I had spent the night with you for devious reasons of my own—reasons I'm still not fully sure of. Although I do know they involve my father, in some way.' She frowned. 'Last night when we met, your attitude towards me had changed yet again. For some reason you announced you wanted to marry me!' She shook her head, not acknowledging for the moment the fact that she had needed to see him again, anyway. His arrogant announcement about marrying her had made null and void any intention she might have had of asking him for the truth about his business dealings with her father. She would rather never know the truth about that than have to be nice to this man! 'You're inconsistent, as well as—'

'Not in the least, Lilli,' he interrupted smoothly, his eyes coolly grey once more. 'The things you just spoke of are the very reasons why I've realised you will make me an excellent wife.'

She became very still. 'I don't see how...'

'I'm under no illusions where you're concerned, Lilli,' he explained. 'I even respect the fact that you tried to help your father—'

'By—as you think—going to bed with you!' Her eyes glittered deeply green at the accusation.

He shrugged. 'By whatever means were at your disposal,' he countered. 'It shows loyalty to your father. And loyalty, if not love, is something to be admired in a wife. My wife,' he added softly.

That word again! She was not going to be his wife, no matter what warped logic he might have used to come to that decision. 'That's no guarantee I would be loyal to you,' she pointed out spiritedly. 'Why should I be? You're arrogant, domineering—'

'So are you,' he mocked in reply.

'And you seem to have some sort of hold over my

father that no one will explain to me!' The last was said almost questioningly.

Patrick's mouth tightened. 'I agree with your father: business is business. Haven't I just explained that these two things are completely separate?'

'You don't "explain" things, Patrick,' she sighed. 'You simply make statements, and expect them to happen!'

He grinned. 'I think that's the first time you've called me Patrick. Plenty of other things, to my face, and otherwise, I suspect.' His grin widened to a smile. 'But never Patrick before.'

'It's your name. But you can be assured I'll never call you husband!' she said vehemently.

He seemed unconcerned. 'Never say never, Lilli. Stranger things have happened. I always said I would never marry again, but you see how wrong I was,' he reasoned patiently.

This man was so exasperating; she was going to scream in a minute! No wonder her father was having problems conducting business with him; he didn't listen to what anyone else had to say. About anything!

She gave an impatient shake of her head. 'Wasn't your first experience at marriage bad enough?' she challenged—and then wished she hadn't as his face darkened ominously. It was obviously still a sensitive subject... And it was also the reason he had no intention of marrying for love... She couldn't help wondering what the beautiful Sanchia had been like as a person, to have created such bitterness in a man as self-assured as Patrick...

'And what do you know of my first marriage?' he said softly—too softly. 'You would have been thirteen when

I married, and sixteen when I divorced—in neither case old enough to be part of that scene.'

Lilli raised her eyebrows. 'You obviously continue to have gossip value, because people are still talking about it!'

'Indeed?' Patrick's voice became frostier. 'And what are these "people" saying about my marriage?'

She looked at him warily; obviously, despite his comment last night about the social gossips, he didn't like the thought that his own life might have been under discussion. 'Only that it didn't work out,' she answered evasively.

He met her gaze compellingly. 'And?'

'What else is there to say?' she said quickly, feeling decidedly uncomfortable now. She wished she had never mentioned his marriage! But she wouldn't have done so if he hadn't come out with that ridiculous statement about marrying her... 'A failed marriage, for whatever reason, is surely a good enough reason not to repeat the experience?'

Patrick gave an assenting nod of his head. 'As is a failed engagement,' he rejoined pointedly.

Lilli felt the heat of resentment in her cheeks. 'Now that isn't open for discussion,' she said sharply.

'Why not?' he taunted. 'The man was a fool. Given the same choices he was, I would have opted for the money *and* you. Although, for my own sake, I'm glad that he didn't.'

Lilli stared at him in frozen fascination. What was he talking about? She and Andy had been engaged for six months when he decided he no longer wanted to marry her, and that in the circumstances he couldn't continue to work for her father, either. It had been a terrible blow at the time, happening, as it did, at the same time as her mother's death. But she had got on with her life, hadn't even seen Andy since the day he broke their engagement. In fact, she had no idea where he was now. And she wasn't interested, either.

Although the comments Patrick had just made about him were rather curious…

'Would you?' she said. 'But then, you're rich in your own right.'

'True,' Patrick conceded dryly. 'Now isn't that a better prospect in a husband than a man who's only interested in embezzling money from your father so that he can go off with his male lover?'

Lilli's stare became even more fixed. He *was* talking about Andy. She knew he was.

Could what he said possibly be true? Had Andy stolen money from her father? Before leaving with *another man*…?

Andy had joined the company as her father's assistant two years ago, a tall blond Adonis, with a charm to match—a charm Lilli, having become disenchanted with the 'let's go to bed' attitude of the men in her social set, had found very refreshing.

She had enjoyed his company too, often finding excuses to visit her father at his office, on the off chance she might bump into Andy there. More often than not, she had, although it had been a few months before he'd so much as invited her to join him for lunch. Over that lunch Lilli had found he was not only incredibly handsome, but also very intelligent, enjoying the verbal challenge of him as well as the physical one.

Looking back, she supposed she had done most of the chasing, but she'd realised it must be awkward for him as she was the boss's daughter. She had followed up that initial lunch with an invitation of her own, so that she might return the hospitality, suggesting the two of them go out to dinner this time. Again Andy had been fun, a witty conversationalist, and again he had behaved like the perfect gentleman when it came time for them to part.

Lilli had been persistent in her interest in him, and after that they'd had dinner together often. That her father approved of the relationship she hadn't doubted; in fact, he'd seemed deeply relieved she was spending so much time with his assistant and less time with her group of friends who seemed to do nothing but party.

Lilli had been thrilled when Andy had asked her to marry him, and if she had been a little disappointed in his continued lack of ardour after their engagement she had accepted that it was out of respect for her, and could ultimately only bode well for their future marriage.

But now Patrick seemed to be saying something else completely, was implying that Andy's lack of physical interest in her hadn't stemmed from respect for her at all, but from the fact that his sexual inclinations lay elsewhere!

He also seemed to be saying that Andy's engagement to her had enabled him to steal from her father's company...

Admittedly, as her father's future son-in-law, Andy had been given more responsibility in the company, and as Lilli's mother's illness had deteriorated Andy had been left more and more in charge of things while her father spent time at home.

Had Andy used that trust in him to take the opportunity to steal from Bennett Hotels?

As she looked at Patrick, the certainty in his gaze, that contemptuous twist to his lips, she knew that was exactly what Andy had done. He had used her to cheat her father…!

The blackness was only on the outer edge of her consciousness at first, and then it seemed to fill her whole being. Darkness. No light. Her legs buckled beneath her as she crumpled to the carpeted floor.

CHAPTER FIVE

LILLIE couldn't focus properly when she opened her eyes, but she did know enough to realise she was no longer on the floor of the dining-room, that someone—and that someone had to be Patrick Devlin!—had carried her through to the adjoining sitting-room and had laid her on the sofa there.

'My God, woman,' he rasped from nearby. 'Don't ever give me a scare like that again!'

He sounded angry—but then, he sounded like that a lot of the time!

What had she—? Why—?

Their conversation suddenly came flooding back in a sickening rush. Andy. Her father. The money...!

She moved to sit up, only to find herself pushed firmly back down once more.

'You aren't moving until I'm sure you aren't going to fall down again!' Patrick ordered as he bent over her, scowling darkly.

His expression alone was enough to make her want to shut her eyes and black out the world again, but even as she wished for that to happen she knew that the terrible truth would still be there when she was conscious again.

'Who else knows?' Her voice was barely audible. 'About Andy, I mean. The money. And—and the other man.' Her fiancé hadn't just walked out on her, which she had thought was bad enough—he had actually gone with another man!

Had the friends she'd spent the last two evenings with

known about that? Had they all been laughing, or pitying her, behind her back? Had they all known that Andy's only reason for being with her at all was so that he had easier access to the Bennett funds? She didn't want to face any of them ever again if that were the case!

'I believe your father has managed to keep all of it in the family.' Patrick's mouth twisted wryly as he moved away from her. 'Besides, I'm more interested in the fact that you obviously didn't know. Not until I just told you. Did you?'

She drew in a shaky breath, sitting up, feeling at too much of a disadvantage lying supine on the sofa. She was at too much of a disadvantage with this man already! 'Obviously not,' she managed coolly. 'Who told you about—about Andy?'

'Gerry,' he said quietly. 'Yesterday. In an effort to warn me off you.'

'Which obviously didn't work,' Lilli returned, their conversation giving her the time she needed to collect her thoughts together—and God knew they had fragmented after Patrick's earlier revelation.

'Obviously not.' Patrick grinned. 'You didn't seem exactly heartbroken to me about the loss of your fiancé—even before you knew the truth about him!'

Too much had happened at that time for her to dwell on Andy's sudden disappearance from her life. Since her mother's death she had got through every day as it arrived; there had been no time to cry for her broken engagement. And now that she knew the truth she felt more like punching Andy on the nose than crying for him! How dared he used her in that way? How dared he abuse her father's trust in him?

She stood up, smoothing her pencil-slim black skirt down over her thighs, straightening her emerald-green cashmere sweater, before moving to stand before the mirror over the fireplace, tidying the wispy tendrils of her hair back into the neat plait that hung down her spine.

She could sense Patrick watching her as she smoothed her hair, could have seen his reflection in the mirror if she had chosen to turn her head slightly—but she didn't.

He and his sister were not 'family', even if her father was involved in an affair with Geraldine, even if Patrick did keep insisting he was going to marry her—and she hated the fact that her father seemed to have confided all of this to his mistress. She hated Geraldine Simms more than she had before because her father had confided in the other woman about Andy's betrayal and yet he hadn't told her!

Because now Patrick Devlin knew about it too...

'I'm afraid I'm busy for lunch today, Patrick.' She turned back to him casually.

His mouth quirked as he looked at her, his gaze mocking. 'And every other day, hmm?' he said knowingly.

Lilli calmly met his eyes. 'It is Christmas,' she shrugged.

But despite the numerous invitations she had received during the last few weeks she hadn't accepted any of them. She hadn't refused them either, had been too listless to bother with them. In view of what she had learned about Andy, she had no intention of accepting them now either. But Patrick Devlin didn't need to know that.

'I'm aware of what time of year it is,' Patrick replied. 'But I didn't think you were.' He looked around at the lack of any Christmas decorations in the room.

Neither she nor her father had felt like putting up a tree or their usual decorations this year. It would be their first Christmas without her mother, and so far neither of them had the heart for seasonal celebrations.

Although now that her father was involved with Geraldine Simms he might feel differently about that; the other woman's home had certainly been highly festooned with decorations at the party two days ago!

Lilli's mouth tightened, her eyes glacially green as she looked across at Patrick. 'We're still in mourning for my mother,' she stated flatly. Although she somehow didn't think her father was any more!

'Caroline.' Patrick nodded in acknowledgement of Lilli's mother. 'I met her several times. Before her illness curtailed her social life. She was a very beautiful woman. You look a lot like her,' he added softly.

Pain flickered in the depths of Lilli's eyes. Somehow it had never occurred to her that this man could have known her mother. Although, as he'd said, until her illness had incapacitated her a year before her death, her mother had been a familiar part of the social scene. Even her illness hadn't robbed her of her incredible beauty, the two of them often able to fool people into believing they were sisters rather than mother and daughter.

'I really do have to get on now, Patrick.' She gave a pointed look at her slender gold wristwatch.

To her chagrin he grinned across at her. 'Miss Bennett has spoken,' he taunted.

Angry colour darkened her cheeks at his continued insistence that she was two people. 'At least she's polite!' she snapped.

'To the point of coldness,' he acknowledged dryly. 'Why aren't you curious to know more about your ex-fiancée, Lilli?' His eyes were narrowed thoughtfully.

Because so much made sense now—Andy's initial reluctance to ask her out, his lack of ardour during their engagement. She didn't want to dwell on those things, felt humiliated enough already!

'My father will tell me anything I need to know,' she dismissed quickly.

Patrick gave a disgusted snort. 'He doesn't seem to have told you very much so far!'

She glared at him. 'My father is very protective of me.' She was positive that was the reason her father hadn't told her about Andy. She had been devastated by her mother's death, and to have learnt of Andy's complete betrayal at the same time would have been unbearable. In fact, the more she thought about it, the more she was sure Andy had chosen his timing for that very reason...! She had felt hurt before, but what she thought of Andy now wasn't even repeatable!

'To the point of stupidity, I now realise,' Patrick countered harshly. 'You simply have no idea.'

She swallowed hard at his accusing tone. She was beginning to realise, and she only loved her father all the more for trying to spare her further pain. Although it seemed to have caused him complications he could well have done without, including, she was sure, being at loggerheads with this man.

'The love of a parent for a child is all-forgiving,' she defended chokily, aware as she said so that it was time this 'child' stopped being cocooned and began to be of some help to her father. He had carried this heavy burden on his own for too long.

Possibly it was the reason he had become involved so quickly with someone so unsuitable as Geraldine Simms...?

In recent years, with her mother so ill, her father had begun to confide in Lilli instead when it came to business matters, but she realised that for the last few months she had been too engrossed in her own pain to give him the attention he had so obviously needed. Which was why he had turned to someone outside the family for comfort.

'And the love of a child for the parent?' Patrick prompted softly.

Lilli gave him a sharp look. This man was too astute; he had guessed she was thinking of her father's involvement with his sister!

'Yes,' she answered unhesitating. She didn't like her father's involvement with Geraldine Simms, but after what she had just learnt of her father's recent worries she was no longer going to give him a hard time over it. She would just have to be around to help pick up the pieces when Geraldine tired of playing with him!

Patrick was still watching her closely. 'Do you like children, Lilli?'

She met his gaze defensively. 'Yes—did you think I wouldn't?' She and Andy had discussed the idea of having—

She and Andy...! How ridiculous the idea of them having children seemed now!

Patrick shrugged. 'You didn't seem too keen earlier when I mentioned having four—'

'I like children, would dearly like some of my own,' Lilli interrupted firmly. 'I just don't intend for them to be yours!'

He looked totally unconcerned by her vehemence. 'But think of the social coup you will have made by getting me to the altar,' he mocked. 'I've made no secret of my contempt for the institution of marriage!'

As Sally had clearly told her last night. Certainly, walking off with the much coveted prize of Patrick Devlin as a husband would more than compensate for the humiliation of having had a fiancé who had left her for another man! But once all the excitement had died down she was the one who would be married to this man, and was a lifetime of his torment really worth that? At this moment in time, she didn't think so!

'Thank you for the offer—but no,' she said crisply.

He looked at her with assessing eyes. 'It won't be open for ever, you know,' he said.

She gave a wry smile. 'I never thought that it would.' She was still dazed he had asked her at all!

His mouth twisted mockingly. 'But the answer is still no?'

'Most definitely,' she agreed forcefully.

'For now,' he said.

Lilli looked at him suspiciously. She was still reeling from the shock of Andy's betrayal, couldn't even think straight yet. But she did know she didn't want to marry this man.

'I really do have things to do, Patrick,' she told him again firmly, wishing he would just leave now so that she could think.

He studied her for several seconds, and then he gave a brief nod. 'I have no doubts our paths will cross again,' he murmured huskily.

She didn't know how he could be so sure. They hadn't met at all in the previous five years. Admittedly, Patrick seemed to have lived in America for most of that time, but he had no doubt been in London on several occasions during those years, if only to see his sister, and Lilli had managed to avoid ever meeting him. The only connection she could see between them now was the business he had with her father, and her father's relationship with his sister.

'Maybe,' she returned enigmatically.

He grinned again. 'But not if you can manage to avoid it!' he guessed.

'We've managed never to meet socially before, so perhaps it would be better if we left it that way,' she told him coolly.

'For whom?' he drawled. 'Having met you, Lilli, I'm in no hurry to lose you again.'

Was he never going to leave? She did have things to do—and going to see her father was top of that list. She intended speaking to him before his meeting with Patrick later this afternoon...

'And please don't say I've never had you to lose,' Patrick went on mockingly. 'You may have chosen to have a convenient memory lapse about the other night, but, believe me, I remember all of it!' he assured her.

She clearly, to her intense mortification, remembered waking up to the sound of him singing happily in the shower yesterday morning; he certainly hadn't sounded like a man dissatisfied with his night! But she hadn't 'chosen' to forget anything; she just didn't, apart from that brief memory flash earlier, remember what had happened between them that first night.

'I'm sure you do,' she dismissed briskly. 'But at the same time I doubt you ask every woman you go to bed with to marry you!'

He raised dark brows. 'In the last five years since my divorce?' he said thoughtfully. 'I think so—yes...' He nodded.

Lilli stared at him. Oh, Sally had said he didn't get involved, but— But Patrick couldn't really be saying she was the first woman he had been to bed with since his divorce. Could he...?

Patrick smiled at her stunned expression. 'It isn't exactly a secret, Lilli. Sanchia taught me never to trust anyone. Especially a woman,' he added hardly. 'And I never have,' he ground out harshly.

She drew in a sharp breath. 'I'm a woman,' she told him shakily.

'Undoubtedly so,' he agreed, touching her lightly on one creamy cheek. 'But I don't have to trust you to marry you. As I've already said, our marriage would be a business arrangement.'

She moved abruptly back from that caressing hand. 'No doubt with a suitable pre-nuptial agreement,' she derided scornfully.

He met her gaze steadily. 'That sort of agreement is only relevant if you intend divorcing each other at some later date. I have no wish to go through another divorce. The next time I marry it will be for life.'

She couldn't break her gaze away from his! She wanted to. Desperately wanted to. But she felt as if she was drowning in the depths of those dark grey eyes. And she knew he meant every word he said...!

She tilted her head back, flicking her plait back over her shoulder. 'No love, no divorce; is that the way it works?' she challenged, wishing she sounded a little more forceful. But she was seriously shaken by the determination of his gaze.

'Exactly.'

Lilli shook her head. 'I find that very sad, Patrick.' She frowned. 'Marriage should be for love.'

'Always?'

'Always,' she echoed firmly.

His mouth twisted. 'You can still say that, after the experience you've just gone through? With your parents' marriage as another shining example of marital bliss?' He shook his head. 'There's scepticism, and then there's stupidity, Lilli, and I'm very much afraid that you—'

'That is enough!' she cried, eyes as hard as emeralds now. 'Leave my parents out of this discussion. You know nothing about them or their marriage. All you know is that my father is now involved with your sister. But it won't last.' Her lips pursed disdainfully. 'Your sister's affairs never do.'

'And your father's affairs?' he taunted.

'My father doesn't have affairs!' Her cheeks were hot with indignation, her hands clenched angrily at her sides. 'Your sister has just caught him on the rebound from my mother's death. He wouldn't have looked at her twice while my mother was alive!' she added heatedly.

Patrick looked at her pityingly. 'Is everything this black and white for you, Lilli? No shades of grey at all?'

'My father brought me up never to accept less than the best,' she told him with passion. 'And so far I never have…!'

Patrick looked at her wordlessly for several long seconds, and then he slowly shook his head. 'And I hope— sincerely hope, Lilli—that you never do,' he murmured. 'And I mean that, Lilli. I really do.'

Somehow she believed him. 'Thank you,' she accepted.

His mouth quirked. 'Now go away?'

She gave a rueful smile. 'Yes.'

He laughed softly. 'I've enjoyed knowing you, Lilli. It's certainly never been boring. See me to the door?' he prompted throatily.

She had intended doing that anyway; as he had already said, she had been brought up to be a good hostess, and telling a guest to find his own way out, no matter who he was, was not polite! Besides, after trying to get him to leave for the last twenty minutes, she wanted to make sure he had actually gone!

'Certainly,' she agreed.

Patrick chuckled as the two of them walked down the hallway to the door, grinning as Lilli turned to him questioningly. 'You're very refreshing, Lilli; as far as I'm aware, you're the first woman who couldn't wait for me to go!' he explained self-derisively.

Not such a perfect hostess, after all! 'I—'

'Have things to do,' he finished for her. 'So you've already said.'

'Several times,' she reminded him playfully, relieved they had at last reached the door.

Patrick turned to her. 'Don't say goodbye, Lilli,' he murmured as she would have spoken. 'You may wish it were, but we both know it isn't.'

She knew no such thing! There was absolutely no reason—

There was no time for further thought as Patrick bent down and kissed her!

And it wasn't a light kiss either, as he pulled her easily into his arms and moulded her body against his.

Lilli felt as if she was drowning, couldn't breathe, was aware of nothing but the possession of this man. And it was complete possession, of the mind, body, and senses.

She could only look up at him with dazed green eyes as he released her as suddenly as he had kissed her.

'No matter what you think to the contrary, neither of us can say goodbye to that, Lilli,' he told her gruffly in parting, the door closing softly behind him as he finally left.

Lilli didn't move, could hear the thunder of her own blood as it rushed around her body. She had been out with men before Andy, quite a few of them, but none of them, including Andy, had evoked the response that Patrick did. It was incredible. Unbelievable.

Dangerous…! How could she respond to a man she
didn't even like very much? For there was no denying
the force of electricity that filled the air whenever they
were together.

Well, despite what Patrick might have claimed to the
contrary, she intended them not to be together again.

'Lilli…?' Her father stood up uncertainly from behind
his desk, his eyes searching as he moved to kiss her
lightly on the cheek in greeting. 'I didn't expect to see
you again until this evening.' He looked at her a little
warily, Lilli thought.

Which wasn't surprising, considering what she had
learnt from Patrick earlier. Her father had carried that
knowledge around with him for months now, and, on
closer inspection, he looked grey with worry. Until today
Lilli had put his gauntness down to the loss of her
mother, but she now realised it was so much more than
that. But she had no intention of letting him worry alone
any longer.

She had been lucky when she'd arrived at his office
a few minutes ago, his secretary able to happily inform
her he was alone, and could see her immediately. Her
father didn't look quite so pleased to see her!

Lilli looked at him with wide, unblinking eyes. 'Exactly how much money did Andy take?' she said evenly.
'And what are you doing about it?'

Her father staggered, as if she had actually hit him,
sitting back down in the leather chair behind his desk,
his face white now, eyes as green as her own gleaming
brightly.

Her own legs felt slightly shaky, she had to admit,
knowing from her father's reaction to those two simple
questions that Patrick had told her the truth about Andy's

disappearance. And, having told her the truth about the money, he no doubt had also told her the truth about whom Andy had gone away with...!

'Oh, Daddy!' She moved around the desk to hug him. 'You should have told me,' she said emotionally.

'No prizes for guessing exactly who did,' he muttered bitterly.

She moved back slightly to look down at him, her own eyes glittering with unshed tears. 'It's irrelevant who did the telling, Daddy. And to give Patrick his due,' she added grudgingly, 'he didn't realise I didn't already know.'

Her father's smile came out as more of a grimace. 'Did he survive the telling unbruised?'

Her mouth twisted at the memory of their conversation. 'Physically, yes. Verbally—probably not.' She shrugged. 'But I'm really not interested in Patrick Devlin's feelings just now; he isn't important.'

'I'm afraid he is, Lilli,' her father sighed. 'Very much so, in fact.'

She moved to sit on the edge of his desk. 'Tell me,' she invited.

It wasn't very pretty in the telling, and for the main part her father avoided meeting her gaze. It was more or less as Lilli had worked out in her own mind; Andy had used her father's preoccupation with his wife's illness to embezzle money from the company.

'How much?' she prompted softly.

'A lot—'

'How much Daddy?' she said forcefully.

He swallowed hard. 'Several million—'

'Several million!' Lilli repeated incredulously. 'Oh, my God...!' she groaned—this was so much worse than she had thought. Her eyes widened. 'That's why Patrick is involved in this, isn't it?' she realised weakly.

Her father scowled darkly. 'He had no right telling you that part,' he rasped harshly.

'He didn't,' she assured him shakily. 'I'm not completely stupid, Daddy; I can add two and two together and come up with the correct answer of four. Andy stole money from you, Patrick is a banker, you are now having difficult business discussions with Patrick; it isn't hard to work out that the two things are connected!'

'I wish to God they weren't!' Her father stood up abruptly, his expression grim. 'The money that Andy took was made through transactions at Cleveley Bank. It had been put in a separate account, ready to pay a loan we took out just over a year ago when we expanded into Australia. The loan was due for repayment two months ago. But when I accessed the account before that I found all the funds had been redirected out of the country,' he recalled heavily, even the memory of it, Lilli could see, bringing him out in a cold sweat.

'Into an account in Andy's name,' she easily guessed.

'Yes,' her father acknowledged dully.

'And Patrick now owns Cleveley Bank,' she said flatly. 'That's why the two of you have been locked in some sort of negotiation.'

Her father nodded. 'And Devlin won't give an inch.'

'But surely if you're prosecuting Andy Patrick can't just—'

'I'm not prosecuting Andy, Lilli,' her father told her.

'What?' she cried. 'But why on earth not? If you bring a case against Andy surely the bank can't— It's because of me, isn't it?' she suddenly realised, becoming very still. 'You haven't charged Andy because you don't want to involve me in this,' she groaned, realising this was what Patrick had meant earlier about the extent of her father's protectiveness of her. Well she knew now, and she had no intention of letting this situation continue. 'Daddy, I know all about Andy, about the money, about—about the other man.' She gave a pained grimace as he looked at her worriedly. 'And when you have your meeting with Patrick this afternoon I want you to tell him you are in the process of bringing a case against Andy. There's no way he can continue to hound you in this way if you're involved in a court case to try and retrieve the money.' Even as she spoke she wasn't sure of the truth of that statement.

She wasn't really sure how her father would stand legally even if he were prosecuting Andy over the theft of the money. And from what she had gathered from Patrick's comments the night she had met him—comments she now understood completely!—his sister's pleadings on behalf of her lover hadn't moved him, so perhaps this was going to make no difference to him either. After all, her father was the one who owed the money, and it probably wasn't the business of the bank if that money had been embezzled...

Her father sighed again wearily. 'Lilli, if I bring charges against Andy, then the whole story will come out.'

'I'm aware of that.'

'And you will end up looking totally ridiculous,' he continued gravely.

Her mouth twisted wryly. 'It won't be the first time!'

'I mean seriously humiliated, Lilli.' Her father shook his head. 'Andy's sexual inclinations are of no interest to anyone at this moment, but they will make headlines when put together with his engagement to you and his embezzling money from me. You would end up a laughing-stock, Lilli, and I won't have that,' he stated determinedly.

'At any price?' she prompted softly.

His mouth tightened stubbornly. 'At any price.'

Her expression softened lovingly, her smile a little shaky. 'I appreciate what you're saying Daddy. And I thank you for your loving protectiveness. But there's really no need,' she added brightly. 'You see, I won't end up a laughing-stock at all. Because I intend marrying Patrick Devlin!'

The answer to the problem was suddenly so simple. As Patrick had said, he was a good catch as a husband— and no one could possibly laugh at her, or pity her over her engagement to Andy, when she had managed to captivate such an eligible man as Patrick Devlin.

There was also the additional fact that, although Geraldine's pleadings on her lover's behalf might have fallen on stony ground, Patrick could hardly appear callous enough to the business world as to actually hound his own father-in-law.

Her marriage to Patrick was the answer to all their problems...

CHAPTER SIX

'LILLI!' Geraldine Simms looked totally stunned as her maid showed Lilli into her sitting-room. She stood, very beautiful in slim-fitting black trousers and an even more fitted black jumper, her hair a tumble of deep red onto her shoulders and down her spine, her expression of surprise turning to one of wariness. 'What can I do for you?' she asked slowly.

Lilli steadily returned the other woman's stare, seeing Geraldine as men must see her—as her own father must see her! She was a self-assured woman of thirty-two, and there was no doubting Geraldine's beauty—almost as tall as Lilli, with that gorgeous abundance of red hair, eyes of deep blue, her face perfectly sculptured.

No wonder her father was smitten!

Lilli mouth tightened as she thought of Geraldine's relationship with her father. 'You can tell me where I might find Patrick,' she said abruptly. Contacting the man seemed to be her problem at the moment, and as her father had refused to tell her where Patrick's office was Lilli had had no choice but to come to Geraldine.

In fact, her father was proving altogether difficult at the moment where Patrick was concerned. Richard Bennett had been horrified by her announcement that she intended marrying Patrick, and had flatly refused to have any part of it when Lilli had proved stubbornly decided on the matter, to the point where he wouldn't even tell her where he was meeting with Patrick this afternoon. So, much as Lilli had wanted to avoid the other woman,

Geraldine had seemed the obvious source—was sure to know, as he was a guest in her home, where her brother was.

'Patrick?' Geraldine looked even more startled. 'Why do you want to see Patrick?'

Lilli stiffened. She hadn't relished the idea of coming here at all, wished there were some other way of contacting Patrick; she certainly didn't intend to engage in a dialogue with Geraldine! 'I believe that's between Patrick and myself,' she returned coolly. The pluses of accepting Patrick's proposal far outweighed the minuses, but at the top of the minuses was definitely the fact that this woman was his sister!

Geraldine shook her head. 'Lilli—'

'I believe Lilli said it was private between the two of us, Gerry,' Patrick interjected as he strolled into the room, wearing a dark blue business suit and white shirt now, obviously dressed for the office. 'Did you decide to accept my lunch invitation, after all?' He turned enquiringly to Lilli.

'Yes,' she agreed thankfully. She hadn't actually expected him to be here, had no intention of accepting his marriage proposal in front of his sister. She had never been so pleased to see him!

'Fine.' He took a firm hold of Lilli's arm. 'See you later, Gerry,' he added dismissively, turning Lilli firmly toward the door.

'But—'

'Later, Gerry,' Patrick repeated hardly.

Lilli released her arm from Patrick's grip as soon as they were outside, silent as he unlocked his car before opening the door for her to get inside. She was silent, because at this moment she couldn't think of anything to say. Now that she was actually face to face with

Patrick again, the enormity of what she was about to do was quite mind-boggling. How could she agree to be this man's wife, bear his children? But, by the same token, how could she not?

'Save it until we get to the restaurant.' Patrick reached out and briefly clasped her clenched hands as they lay in her lap, his eyes never wavering from the road ahead. 'I booked a table for one o'clock.'

She turned to him sharply. 'You booked...? You knew I would have lunch with you all the time?' Anger sharpened her voice.

'I—hoped that you would change your mind,' he answered carefully.

He had known she would have lunch with him after all. What else did he know...?'

Lilli gave him an assessing look before turning her head to stare rigidly out of the front windscreen. She felt as a mouse must do when being tormented by a cat— and she didn't like the feeling any more than the mouse did! This man always seemed to be one step ahead of her, and in a few short minutes she was going to agree to be his wife. What on earth was her life going to be like, married to him?

Even the restaurant he had chosen had been picked with privacy in mind, each table secluded in its own booth, the service quietly discreet as they were shown to one, Patrick obviously known here as he was greeted with obsequious politeness; Lilli, as his guest, was treated with that same solicitousness.

'Is it too early to order champagne?' Patrick asked her lightly as the waiter hovered for their drinks order.

Lilli's chin rose defiantly, she might be down, but she wasn't defeated! 'As long as it's pink,' she told him haughtily. 'I never drink any other sort of champagne.'

Patrick's mouth twisted wryly. 'I'll try to remember that.' He turned to the waiter. 'A bottle of your best pink champagne,' he ordered.

'I don't think I've ever been here before.' Lilli gave a bored look round the room once they were alone again, noting how it was impossible, from the angle at which the booths were placed, to see any of the other people dining at the adjoining tables. 'It looks like the ideal place for a man to bring his mistress without fear of them being seen together,' she added scathingly.

Patrick smiled at her description. 'I wouldn't know,' he drawled, also looking casually about them. 'But you could be right.' He turned back to her. 'The food is excellent.' He indicated she should look at the menus they had been given.

Lilli looked at him for several long seconds, until she could withstand the laughter in his eyes no longer. 'The food,' she finally conceded, looking down at her menu.

'And the company,' Patrick added softly. 'Just Lilli,' he murmured huskily.

And she had been trying so hard to be Elizabeth Bennett. Damn him!

Her mouth tightened. 'Let's just get this over—'

'The champagne, Lilli,' he cut in softly, drawing her attention to the waiter waiting to pour their bubbling wine.

She drew in a ragged breath, sitting back in her seat while the champagne was poured into their glasses. She really did just want to get this over with now, and these constant interruptions weren't helping her at all.

Patrick raised his glass in a toast as soon as their glasses were full. 'To us, Lilli,' he stated firmly. 'Or am I being a little premature?' he prompted as she made no move to pick up her own glass.

'How long have you known?' she said heavily. 'That I would marry you,' she explained as he raised questioning brows.

He shrugged. 'I told you last night as we danced, but I suppose I actually realised the merits of it after I had left you yesterday afternoon—'

'I mean, how long have you known I would marry you?' she cut in impatiently, glaring at him frustratedly.

'Oh, that.' He sipped his champagne before glancing down at his menu.

'Yes—that,' she bit out tautly. 'You really are the most arrogant, infuriating—'

'I love it when you talk to me like that.' He grinned. 'No one else does, you know. Except Gerry, and— I realise you don't even like the mention of her name.' He frowned and she flinched. 'But she is my sister, and as such will become your sister-in-law once we're married.'

Lilli met his remark coldly. 'Even so, I don't see that I have to have anything to do with her.'

'Lilli—'

'I mean it, Patrick,' she told him. 'I accept your marriage proposal—but it won't all be on your terms!'

'I never for a moment thought it would—'

'Oh, yes, you did.' Her eyes flashed deeply green. 'But you chose me because of the person I am, and that means the whole person; no matter what you think to the contrary, Lilli and Elizabeth Bennett are not two divisible people—and neither of them wants anything to do with your sister!'

'Hmm, this is difficult,' Patrick murmured thoughtfully.

'Not as difficult as trying to pretend the two of us will

ever accept each other! She's your sister. I will be your
wife. The two of us—'

'I wasn't referring to that situation,' Patrick dismissed
with a wave of his hand. 'I simply don't know whether
to have the salmon or the pheasant for lunch.' He pursed
his lips thoughtfully as he studied the menu once again.

Lilli stared at him incredulously. Did nothing trouble
this man? Did he make a joke out of everything?

'No, Lilli, I don't,' he murmured softly as if reading
her mind, reaching out to clasp one of her hands with
his as it lay on the table-top. 'Close your mouth, my
darling, and stop upsetting yourself,' he teased. 'The
problem between you and Gerry will sort itself out in its
own good time. You're both adult women. And I have
no intention of interfering.'

Lilli wasn't incredulous any more, she was stunned.
'Darling'. He had called her his 'darling'… And as her
husband he would have a perfect right to call her any
endearment he pleased. He would have the right to do a
lot more than that!

She hastily removed her hand from beneath his. 'I
want a long engagement—'

'No,' he cut in calmly, to all intents and purposes still
studying his menu.

Colour heightened her cheeks. 'I told you this isn't
going to be all on your terms,' she reminded him tautly.

He gave a brief nod. 'And I agreed it wouldn't,' he
said. 'But a long engagement is out of the question. With
a special licence we can be married before Christmas.'

Lilli gasped. 'Before—! You can't be serious,' she
protested, sitting forward. 'It's only nine days away; I
can't possibly be ready to marry you between now and
then!'

'Of course you can,' he assured her smoothly. 'Now

I suggest we order our meal,' he added pleasantly as the waiter approached their table. 'I have a meeting at three o'clock,' he reminded her.

His meeting was with her father. They really didn't have the time before that meeting to sort this out properly. She couldn't decide on the rest of her life in an hour and a half!

'I haven't even had a chance to read the menu yet,' she told him dully; she had looked at it, but she hadn't actually read it.

'Another few minutes,' he told the waiter pleasantly.

Lilli shook her head. 'I'm really not hungry.'

Grey eyes looked compellingly into hers. 'You have to eat, Lilli.'

She swallowed hard. 'I really don't think I can—'

'Avocado salad and the salmon,' Patrick told the waiter decisively. 'For both of us.' He turned back to Lilli once they were alone again. 'I'll agree to any other terms you care to suggest, Lilli,' he offered. 'But the timing of our marriage is not for negotiation.' His mouth tightened. 'I have no intention of your father settling his problem with Andrew Brewster—and you breaking our engagement so fast you end up bruising yourself in your speed to get my ring off your finger!' His eyes glittered coldly as he looked at her between narrowed lids.

'A 'barracuda in a city suit' was how her father had described this man—and how right he was. Breaking off the engagement was exactly what she had been hoping to do! She really didn't want to be married to this man, had hoped—oh, God, she had hoped her father would be able to solve his financial problems without her actually having to go through with marriage to Patrick Devlin.

She should have known Patrick would see straight through any ideas like that!

Her head went back proudly, her eyes glittering brightly. 'I suppose you've decided what I'm to wear for this wedding, too?'

'White, of course, Lilli.' He sipped his champagne, surveying her over the rim of his glass. 'Or are you telling me you don't have the right to wear that colour?' he challenged tauntingly.

'You can ask that, after the other night?' she scoffed.

'Our night together?'

'Of course our night together! Or doesn't it count if the bridegroom was the lover?'

Patrick looked at her thoughtfully for several long seconds. 'I think I should make one thing plain, Lilli,' he finally said. 'My first marriage, after the initial honeymoon period, was a battleground. It's not an experience I care to repeat!'

'Then why choose to marry someone you don't love and who doesn't even pretend to love you?' Lilli asked sceptically.

'Respect, Lilli. I have respect for you, for the love and loyalty you've shown towards your father—'

'A love that gives you the leverage to pressurise me into marrying you!' she accused heatedly.

His facial muscles tightened. 'I believe we both said we would keep my business with your father out of this?'

'You don't honestly think I would give marrying you a second thought if it weren't for that, do you?' She shook her head scathingly.

'It wasn't mentioned in the proposal. And I don't believe it was mentioned in the acceptance?' He raised dark brows pointedly.

'It may not have been mentioned, but—'

'Let's leave it that way, hmm?' His voice was dangerously soft now.

Lilli surveyed him mutinously, silenced by the coldness in his voice. But he couldn't seriously expect her to act as if she were in love with him? That would be asking the impossible!

She drew in a ragged breath. 'Patrick—'

'Our food, Lilli.' He sat back as the avocado was placed in front of them.

This was ridiculous. They couldn't possibly discuss something as important as the rest of their lives over lunch, with the constant interruptions that entailed. How on earth did he think—?

'Try the avocado, Lilli,' Patrick encouraged gently. 'I think we might both feel a little more—comfortable, once we've eaten something.'

She very much doubted this man knew what it was like to feel uncomfortable. But he was probably right about the food settling her ragged nerves; she hadn't eaten anything at all today. The only problem with that was that her stomach was churning so much she wasn't sure she would keep the food inside her if she ate it!

'Try it, Lilli.' Patrick held a forkful of his own avocado temptingly in front of her mouth.

She gave him a startled glance, slightly alarmed by his close proximity. But the determined look in his eyes told her he wasn't about to move away until she took the avocado from the fork he held out.

'This is ridiculous,' she muttered as she moved slightly forward to take the food into her mouth. 'Anyone would think we were a couple really in love,' she added irritably before moving back from him, picking up her own fork to eat her meal.

'Better?' He nodded his satisfaction with her compliance.

She had to admit, inwardly, that the food was indeed excellent, and it wasn't choking her as she had thought it might—but Patrick treating her as a recalcitrant child was! 'Don't treat me like a six-year-old, Patrick—'

'Then don't act like one,' he came back swiftly. 'I certainly don't want a temperamental child for a wife! Think, Lilli,' he continued hardly. 'Your father—does he know you've come to accept my proposal…?'

She swallowed. 'Yes.'

'And?'

'And what?' She frowned her tension.

Patrick's mouth twisted mockingly. 'And he's ecstatic at your choice of husband?' he taunted.

She gave a snort. 'Don't be ridiculous—'

'Exactly,' Patrick acknowledged dryly. 'As Gerry is going to be overjoyed at my choice of wife!'

Lilli stiffened. 'I'm really not interested in how your sister feels about me.'

'And your father's approval is of little importance to me, either,' he returned. 'But, if I'm correct in my assumption concerning your reasons for accepting my proposal, after all, then it's primarily to help your father, but also because once your father prosecutes Brewster the man's private life is bound to become public knowledge. But you will obviously have caught a much bigger fish on your marital hook, and so have no fear of becoming the object of the scorn or gossip that could ensue. Stop me if I'm wrong—'

'You know you aren't!' she snapped resentfully; did this man know everything? 'But exactly where is all this leading to?' she prompted impatiently.

'This is leading to the fact…' he deliberately held

another morsel of avocado temptingly in front of her, leaning intimately forward as he did so '…that our engagement, and subsequent marriage, will be more believable to everyone, including your father and my sister, if it seems that we are genuinely in love with each other.'

Lilli stared at him as if he had gone insane—because at that moment it seemed he actually might be! No one could possibly believe the two of them really loved each other, least of all her father.

'Without that belief, Lilli,' Patrick continued, 'everyone will know the whole thing is a sham—and you will end up looking more foolish than if this whole thing had become public months ago!'

He was right… Once again he was right! Why hadn't she thought of that? Because she hadn't been thinking at all, only feeling, and this marriage to Patrick had seemed to solve everything.

She swallowed hard. 'What do you suggest?'

His mouth quirked. 'That you eat this avocado; it's in danger of falling off my fork!'

She was in danger of being at the centre of the biggest social farce to become public in years!

She ate the avocado, knowing as she did so exactly what she was committing herself to. The avocado, for all Patrick was making light of it, represented something so much more than a morsel of food. It took all of her will-power to chew it and actually swallow it down.

Patrick touched her cheek gently. 'I'm willing to give this a try if you are, Lilli.'

What choice did she have? She wanted her father to do something about the money that had been taken from his company, and for that to happen the whole thing had to become public. And it would only work if she and Patrick had a believable relationship.

She drew in a ragged breath. 'I'm not sure I can,' she told him honestly.

'I'll try and make it easy for you.' He leant forward and brushed his lips against hers. 'There, that wasn't so difficult, was it?'

He was so close, his breath was lightly ruffling the hair at her temples. So close she could see the dark flecks of colour in his grey eyes. So close she could smell the elusiveness of his aftershave. So close she couldn't stop the slight trembling of her knees, the tight feeling in her chest, the disruption of her breathing.

'Not so difficult,' she admitted gruffly.

'And do you agree it will be better than people thinking we hardly know each other?' he teased.

That was the last thing she wanted! 'I agree.'

'The wedding will be next week—I thought a three out of three in the agreeing department was expecting a bit much!' He grinned as she looked panicked at the suggestion. 'It will fit in with the idea of a whirlwind romance,' he explained. 'Everyone loves a romance, Lilli—especially if it appears a love-match!'

Her stomach had given a sickening lurch at the very thought of being married to this man in only a matter of days. She swallowed hard. 'That sounds—reasonable.' What difference did it make? Patrick intended them to be married, had no intention of her dragging out their engagement in the hope she might never need to tie the knot. So she might as well get on with it!

He sat back so that their plates could be taken away— and allowed Lilli to breathe again!

This man was going to be her husband. They would live together. Patrick would come to know her body more intimately than she knew it herself. He—

She was panicking again! Take each step as it comes!

she told herself. If she looked at the whole thing she would become hysterical. Yes, that was it; she just had to take each day, each step, as it arrived. She would be fine. After all—

'Make sure you have a white dress for the wedding, Lilli.' Patrick interrupted her thoughts. 'I'm aware you've been desperately trying to forget the night we spent together, but—'

'Please,' she hastily cut in. 'That night was completely out of character. I have never done anything like that before, and—'

'And you haven't done anything like that now, either, Lilli,' Patrick dismissed mockingly.

'How can you possibly say that?' She shook her head in self-disgust. 'I—'

'You were very beautiful that night, Lilli, very alluring, and I have to admit that, for the first time in years, I was physically interested. And I would probably have been only too happy to enjoy all the pleasure you were so obviously promising. Unfortunately—' he shook his head dramatically '—the champagne and wine took their toll on you, and you fell asleep on the bed in the hotel while I was in the bathroom.'

Lilli stared at him, not sure she was hearing him correctly.

He laughed softly at her stunned expression. 'I can see you're having trouble believing me. But I can assure you it's the truth.'

'But I—I was undressed,' she protested disbelievingly. She could clearly remember her embarrassment the next morning when she'd woken up to find she was only wearing her lace panties!

He nodded. 'You most certainly were. And you have a very beautiful body. But the only reason I know that,

the reason you were undressed, is because I couldn't let
you spoil that beautiful gown you were wearing. You
looked lovely in it, and I'd like to see you in it again
one day. You were asleep, so I simply took the dress off
you and settled you more comfortably beneath the bedclothes.'

'And you—where did you sleep?' She was still reeling
from the shock of realising she hadn't made love with
this man at all.

But that memory flashback she had had...? She
couldn't have dreamt being in his arms, being kissed by
him, caressed by him—could she?

Patrick smiled. 'There was only the one double bed
in the bedroom, Lilli, and I have to admit I'm not that
much of a gentleman; I slept beside you, of course. And
very cuddly you were too. In fact, you became quite
charmingly friendly at about four o'clock in the morning,' he added wistfully. 'But there was no way I could
make love to a woman who was too much asleep still
to know where she was, let alone who she was with—'

'Stop it!' she cut in sharply. 'What you're saying is
incredible.' She shook her head dazedly. 'How do I
know you're telling the truth?' She frowned her uncertainty.

He gestured carelessly. 'What reason do I have to lie?
It wouldn't do my reputation any good at all if it became
public knowledge that I'd spent the whole night in bed
with you and didn't even attempt to make love to you!
Although, in retrospect, I can't say I'm disappointed by
the fact. Unless I'm very much mistaken,' he continued
at her questioning look, 'you have more right than most
to wear white on your wedding day. And our wedding
night will be the first time you've ever made love with

any man. I feel very privileged that I'm going to be that man,' he added huskily.

This was incredible. Unbelievable…! But, as Patrick had so rightly pointed out, what reason could he possibly have for lying about it?

But until just now he had let her continue to think— Knew what she had believed had happened between them, and he hadn't disabused her of that belief.

She really had thought she had made love with this man two nights ago, had had no reason to think otherwise. And Patrick had perpetuated that belief with his remarks after that night, had known how she hated the idea of having gone to bed with him in that reckless way. He had continued to let her believe it…

Because it suited him to. Because he had enjoyed watching her discomfort over an incident she would rather forget had happened.

And she had just agreed to marry this man, to live with him, to bear his children. All four of them!

She had, she now realised, made a pact with the devil himself!

CHAPTER SEVEN

'I BELIEVE we have guests coming to dinner this evening?' Lilli's father addressed her stiffly when he came in from his office a little after six; Lilli was in the day-room pretending to be interested in a magazine.

Pretending, because she couldn't really concentrate on anything at the moment!

How she had got through the rest of the lunch with Patrick, she had no idea. She vaguely remembered him talking about trivial things through the rest of their meal, seeming unconcerned with her monosyllabic answers, putting her in a taxi at two forty-five, so that he could go to his meeting with her father. His parting comment, she now remembered, had been something about them dining together this evening, so that her father could get used to the idea of him as a son-in-law.

But, however long his meeting with her father had taken, Patrick had somehow also found the time to call a prestigious newspaper and have notice of their forthcoming marriage put in the classifieds!

Lilli knew all about this because a reporter from the newspaper had telephoned her here just over an hour ago wanting further information on their whirlwind romance. Lilli's answer to this had been, 'No comment.' But not ten minutes later Sally had also telephoned to find out if it was true; it seemed a friend of a friend also worked on the newspaper, and, knowing Sally was a friend of Lilli's, had telephoned her for information. Which Sally couldn't give, thank goodness—because she didn't know any of the details of Lilli's relationship with Patrick!

There was no doubt that Patrick was going to give her no chance for second thoughts, was making this marriage a foregone conclusion by publicly announcing it.

Not that Lilli could have had second thoughts even if she had wanted to. But, Patrick being Patrick, he had made sure that she couldn't, not without causing even more publicity for herself.

She looked up at her father with dull green eyes, noting how strained he looked, matching her own dark mood of despair. 'Guest,' she corrected flatly.

'Guests,' her father insisted as he came further into the room, moving to the tray of drinks on the side table, pouring himself a liberal amount of whisky, swallowing half of the liquid down in one needy gulp. 'Patrick is bringing Gerry with him,' he told Lilli abruptly before swallowing the remaining contents of the glass he held.

This information brought Lilli out of her mood of despondency, her eyes now sparkling angrily. 'He is not bringing that woman to this house,' she stated furiously. 'I told him earlier exactly how I felt about his sister. He knows that I—'

'Lilli, Gerry isn't only Patrick's sister, she's the woman in my life,' her father cut in carefully. 'And while you might have strong feelings about that—in fact, I'm sure you do!—I would rather not hear them.'

'But—'

'I mean it, Lilli,' he told her in a voice that brooked no further argument. 'Now, as my banker, Patrick has advised that I go ahead with bringing a case against Andy for embezzlement,' he continued without a pause. 'He also told me the two of you are to be married before Christmas!'

Lilli's anger against Geraldine Simms left her so suddenly she felt like a deflated balloon. 'If that's what Patrick says, then it must be true,' she told him dryly.

'Lilli—'

'It's what I want, Daddy.' She stood up forcefully, moving restlessly about the room, tidying objects that didn't really need tidying.

'Do you also want to go and live in New York?' he asked.

'New York...?' Lilli stopped her restless movements, staring at her father. 'Did you say New York?'

Her father nodded. 'It's where Patrick is based. His business in England is almost concluded,' he added bitterly. 'He'll be returning to New York in the New Year. And, as his wife, you will go with him.'

She had to admit, she hadn't given much thought to where they would live after their wedding; she was still having trouble coming to terms with the idea of marrying Patrick at all! But New York...! She had completely forgotten he was based in America...

'Lilli, you haven't really thought this thing through at all,' her father sighed as he saw her confused expression. 'You don't even know anyone in New York.'

Except Patrick...

'You'll be all alone over there,' her father continued quietly.

Except for Patrick...

'There will be no one there to love and take care of you,' her father added in a wavering voice.

Except Patrick...!

This was turning out to be worse than she had realised. Her father was right; she hadn't really thought it through at all, had just been looking for a solution to their immediate problems. The long term was something she hadn't really considered.

'Did Patrick tell you we would be going to New York?' she enquired.

'No, it was Gerry who thought of it—I called in to see her on my way home from the office,' he explained defensively as Lilli looked troubled.

Which explained why he was home later than usual. Geraldine had really got her claws into him, hadn't she?

'She's as worried as I am about your marriage to Patrick,' her father told her harshly.

Lilli stiffened. 'Well, thank her for her concern, but I'm quite capable of making my own decisions—and living with the consequences of them, even a move to New York.' She walked angrily to the door, wrenching it open. 'I think you underestimate my ability to adapt to living in New York. I'm sure I'll have a wonderful time. Now, if you'll excuse me, I have to go and change for dinner.' She closed the door firmly behind her.

How dared her father discuss her with that woman? How dared he?

'You look very beautiful,' Patrick told her huskily.

He had arrived at the house with his sister only minutes ago, the four of them in the sitting-room, Lilli's father busy with the dispensing of drinks, the beautiful Gerry already at his side. There was no doubt the other woman *was* beautiful, or that Lilli's father obviously thought so too—he seemed to have come quite boyishly alive in her company. Lilli hated even seeing the two of them together!

'Thank you.' She distantly accepted the compliment, very aware of the other couple in the room.

'As usual,' Patrick added softly.

Lilli turned to look at him, a contemptuous movement to her lips. 'You don't have to keep this up when it's just the two of us, Patrick!'

'But it isn't just the two of us.' He looked pointedly across the room at her father and his sister.

She drew in a ragged breath. 'My father would see straight through any effort on my part to pretend I'm in love with you.'

'Then I would advise you to try a little harder,' Patrick told her hardly. 'Unless you want to cause him even more grief! Andy Brewster was *your* fiancé, Lilli,' he callously reminded her.

As if to confirm Patrick's words, her father glanced worriedly across at the two of them, Lilli forcing a reassuring smile before turning back to Patrick. 'You don't play fair,' she told him in a muted voice.

'I don't "play" at all, Lilli,' he corrected her harshly. 'You should have realised that by now!'

Her eyes flashed her resentment. 'Is that the reason you've already sent the announcement of our marriage to that newspaper?'

Patrick didn't seem at all surprised at her accusation. 'I'm not even going to ask how you know about that; the London gossip grapevine must be one of the busiest in the world! But talking of our marriage...I have a present for you,' he tacked on gently.

She didn't want presents from him; she wished she didn't want anything at all from him!

'Don't look so alarmed, Lilli.' He pretended to chide her. 'This is perfectly in keeping with our new relationship. Ah, Richard, perfectly on cue with the champagne,' he greeted the other man as he held out the two glasses of bubbly pink liquid. 'I was just about to give Lilli her engagement ring.'

An engagement ring! There had been no mention of an engagement, only the wedding. She couldn't—

'We can change it if you don't like it, Lilli,' Patrick assured her as he took the small blue ring-box from his jacket pocket, flicking open the lid to show her the contents.

If she didn't like it! How could any woman not like such a ring? It was beautiful, the hugest emerald Lilli had ever seen surrounded by twelve flawless small diamonds.

Lilli had never seen a ring like it before, let alone been offered such a beautiful piece of jewellery; the ring Andy had given her on their engagement, a ring she had discarded to the back of a drawer when their engagement had ended, had been a diamond solitaire, delicate, unobtrusive. Patrick was intent on making a statement with this magnificent emerald and diamond ring. Of ownership. 'Oh, Patrick,' Gerry breathed in an awestruck voice. 'It's absolutely beautiful!'

He replied ruefully, 'I believe that should be Lilli's line.'

Maybe it would be—if she could actually speak. But all she could do was stare at the ring. It was too much. Just too much. It must have cost a small fortune!

She had been brought up within a well-off family, could never remember being denied anything she had ever wanted, but this ring, and what it must have cost, had suddenly brought home to her exactly how wealthy Patrick was. Such wealth was, in its own way, quite frightening. And she was about to marry into it!

'You don't like it,' Patrick said, his gaze narrowed on the sudden paleness of her face.

She moistened dry lips. 'It isn't that...'

'Richard, you mentioned showing me the Turner you have in the dining-room?' Geraldine prompted.

Lilli looked sharply at the other woman, her mouth tightening at the obvious ease of the relationship between this handsome woman and her own father. 'There's no need to leave Patrick and I alone, Geraldine,' she announced. 'We aren't about to have an argument.'

She had to admit, for a few minutes she had been thrown totally by the ring Patrick had bought for her, but that one glance at how close Geraldine was standing to her father was enough to shake her out of that. Yes, the ring was beautiful. Yes, it had cost a small fortune. But then, Patrick Devlin wouldn't expect his future wife to wear anything but the best. The very best. The ring wasn't actually for her, it was for Patrick Devlin's fiancée—who just happened to be her. Once she had all that sorted out in her mind, there was no problem.

'Of course I like it, Patrick,' she assured him lightly. 'Any woman would,' she added with cool dismissal.

His eyes glittered dangerously. 'I'm not interested in "any woman's" opinion, Lilli,' he rasped. 'I wanted *you* to like it. I should obviously have let you choose it yourself.' He snapped the ring-box shut. 'We'll go out tomorrow and look at some others—'

'You chose this ring, Patrick.' She grasped his wrist to stop him putting the blue velvet box back in his pocket.

He looked down at the paleness of her slender fingers against his much darker skin, before slowly bringing his gaze back to her face.

Lilli withstood his probing assessment of her unflinchingly—although she couldn't say she wasn't relieved when he finally smiled. She couldn't have held his gaze for much longer, would have had to look away. 'The ring, Patrick,' she reminded him chokily.

'Only if you're sure it's what you want.' His smile had gone again now; that harshness was back in his face.

'I'm sure.' There was a challenge in her voice, and she slowly released his wrist, leaving the next move to him.

'Well, I'm not sure I am,' her father asserted. 'This whole thing is ridiculous—'

'The ring is absolutely gorgeous, Daddy.' Lilli smoothly stopped what she was sure was going to be her father's tirade.

'Lilli, you have no idea what you're doing,' he told her exasperatedly. 'You don't have to do—'

'Daddy!' She silenced him. 'Let's drink our champagne. After all, this is supposed to be a celebration.'

'I see nothing to celebrate!' Her father slammed down the glasses he had been holding for them. 'In fact—'

'Richard, I really would like to see that Turner.' Geraldine was the one to interrupt this time, taking a determined hold of his arm.

For long moments it looked as if Lilli's father would refuse, and then he acquiesced with an abrupt nod of his head, his back rigid as he and Geraldine left the room.

'I gather he doesn't approve of your choice of husband?' Patrick drawled softly as he watched the other man depart.

Lilli looked at him with flashing green eyes. 'Did you honestly expect him to?'

Patrick shrugged. 'I think he could be a little more understanding of what you're doing—'

'Understanding!' she echoed scathingly. 'I think he's too angry and upset at the moment to understand anything!'

'I did warn you he would need convincing this marriage was something you really want.'

'And just how am I supposed to do that?' she scorned. 'You can't be trusted, Patrick. You totally deceived me about that night we spent together—'

'That really rankles, doesn't it?' he mocked.

'Of course it rankles!' She had thought of little else since parting from him this afternoon. 'You—'

'Would you rather we had spent the whole night making mad, passionate love to each other?' he taunted.

'Of course not!' Her cheeks went hot with embarrassment just at the thought of it.

'Of course not,' he mimicked softly, suddenly very close. 'Lilli, your first time should be gentle and sensitive. Special. Not a night you don't even remember!'

She swallowed hard, moved, in spite of herself, by the seduction in his voice. 'You still lied to me—'

'When I said you were a ten?' he supplied.

Her blushed deepened. 'About the whole thing! You—'

'I never lied, Lilli,' he assured her. 'I never lie. Remember that,' he added. 'Because I expect the same honesty from the people I deal with.'

Especially wives! God, Sanchia had to have been incredibly brave—or incredibly stupid!—to have deceived this man.

'You're beautiful, Lilli.' He touched her cheek gently, his fingers trailing lightly down her throat to the milky softness of her slightly exposed breasts in the close-fitting black dress she wore. 'You respond to my lightest touch,' he murmured in satisfaction as she trembled. 'I know we're going to be physically compatible.'

Her skin felt on fire where his fingers had caressed. 'A ten...' she murmured weakly.

'Perfect,' he corrected her firmly. 'I only made that remark that day because I was damned angry with you and what I thought you had done. I don't give scores on sexual performance, Lilli. I'm sure I made it plain to you there haven't been any women since I parted from Sanchia five years ago?'

'You said as much, yes...'

'If I said it, then it's the truth,' he bit out harshly.

'Patrick Devlin doesn't lie!'

'You know, Lilli,' he said with pleasant mildness, 'I'm getting a little tired of having to deal with your temper—'

'I never knew I had one until I met you!' she returned heatedly.

'You mean no one ever said no to you until me,' he derided.

He was mocking her again now. And that just made her more angry than ever!

She looked at him defiantly. 'I don't want to live in New York after we're married,' she stated—and then wondered where on earth it had come from. She hadn't meant to say that in anger at all, had intended discussing it with him calmly and reasonably. The problem with that was, she never felt calm and reasonable when she was with him!

'I don't think it's right to discuss that now, Lilli,' he dismissed predictably. 'Stop fighting me over everything, woman,' he ordered as he pulled her into his arms. 'And then maybe we can both start enjoying this!'

Enjoy being with this man? Enjoy being held by him? Enjoy being kissed by him!

Because he was kissing her. Again. And, as on those other occasions when he had kissed her, her body suddenly felt like liquid fire, her legs turning to jelly, so that she clung to his shoulders as the kiss deepened, Patrick's lips moving erotically against hers, his tongue moving lightly over the sensitivity of her inner lip. Lilli moaned low in her throat as he did so.

'Good God…!'

It was her father's shocked outburst that intruded into the complete intimacy of the moment, and it was with some reluctance that Lilli dragged her mouth away from Patrick's, turning slowly to look dazedly in her father's direction.

'Don't look so shocked, Richard.' Patrick was the one to break the awkward silence. 'I realise you have some strange ideas about the reason Lilli and I are to be married, but as you've just witnessed—only too fully!—one of those reasons is that we are very attracted to each other. Haven't you ever heard of "love at first night"?'

Lilli ignored the pun, recovering her senses a lot slower than Patrick had. But with their return came the realisation that Patrick must have heard the other couple's impending return—and this show of passion had been all for their benefit, so that Geraldine and her father would believe the two of them were seriously in love!

If her father's nonplussed expression was anything to go by, it had succeeded! Why shouldn't it have done? Lilli was able to visualise all too easily—to her acute discomfort!—exactly the scene of intimacy her father and Geraldine had just walked in on. She had obviously been a more than willing recipient of Patrick's kisses and caresses!

'It happens this way sometimes, Richard,' Patrick continued, his arm like a steel band about Lilli's waist as he secured her to his side. 'Now that the two of you are back, we can put on Lilli's ring and drink the champagne.'

Lilli watched in a dreamlike state as Patrick slid the ring onto her finger, all the time having the feeling that, once it was on, her fate was sealed.

Who was she trying to fool? Her fate had been sealed from the moment she first met Patrick Devlin.

And as she watched the ring being put on her finger, weighed down by the emerald and diamonds, she knew it was now too late to turn back.

Too late for all of them...

CHAPTER EIGHT

'HOLD still, Lilli, or we'll never get these flowers straight in your hair,' Sally chided lightly.

Lilli stared at her own reflection in the mirror. Hardly the picture of the ecstatic bride on her wedding day!

Oh, the trappings were all there—the white dress, her hair in long curls down her spine, the veil waiting on the back of the chair to be put over the flowers Sally was now entwining in her dark curls.

Sally, the friend she had chosen as her attendant. Sally, who had been absolutely astonished to discover the 'gorgeous man', from the night of Gerry Simms' party, was in fact Lilli's father.

If Lilli had been in the mood for humour, she would have found Sally's incredulity funny. It was definitely the first time she had seen her friend lost for words!

'There.' Sally stood back now to admire her handiwork. 'You look absolutely beautiful, Lilli. Breathtaking!'

She did. The white satin dress and long veil made her look like something from a fairy tale.

Except she wasn't marrying Prince Charming.

She was marrying Patrick Devlin.

Her heart still sank just at the thought of being his wife. It had not been an easy week; Patrick had been at the house constantly as hurried arrangements were made for their wedding. Lilli had given in over everything— the timing of the wedding, the white dress, the private

112

reception later today for family and a few close friends, even the choosing of identical wedding rings.

The one thing she hadn't agreed to—though her father was her choice of witness and Gerry was Patrick's—was Gerry helping her get ready for the wedding. Her mother should have been the one here with her, and as her father's mistress Gerry Simms did not fit the bill! Hence Sally's presence instead.

Thirty more minutes and Lilli and Patrick would be husband and wife. She would be Mrs Patrick Devlin.

As far as Sally—and most of London, it seemed!—was concerned, she should be the happiest woman in the world at this moment.

Happy! She was far from being that. She was going to be married to Patrick, his to do with whatever and whenever he wished. Tonight, they would make love.

God, how she wished she could claim the shiver that ran down her spine at the mere thought of it was caused by revulsion, but she knew in her heart of hearts that it wasn't. The thought of making love with Patrick, of the two of them naked in bed together, entwined in each other's arms, certainly made her quiver—but with anticipation!

Because something else had been happening during the last few days, with Patrick constantly teasing her, bullying her a little, kissing her—oh, yes, the kissing hadn't stopped. In fact, he seemed to take delight in kissing her and touching her whenever the opportunity arose for him to do so. And there seemed to be all too many of those!

To her dismay, Lilli found she was falling in love with him... She had made a pact with the devil—and, to her horror, had found she was falling in love with him!

'What is it, Lilli?' Sally seemed concerned.

From a very long way away, it seemed, Lilli looked up at her dazedly.

'You've gone as white as those tea-roses in your hair,' Sally explained anxiously. 'Lilli, I— Please don't think I'm intruding,' she continued hurriedly, lightly touching Lilli's arm, 'but are you sure you aren't rushing this? I mean, you and Patrick haven't known each other that long, and— Well, he was so very much in love with Sanchia.' She shook her head, looking very good herself in a sleek red suit, blonde hair loose about her slender shoulders. 'I wouldn't want you to be hurt again,' she added worriedly. 'Andy was such a swine to walk out on you the way he did, and I—'

'I don't want to talk about Andy,' Lilli interjected; without Andy's involvement in her family, today wouldn't be happening at all! 'And I appreciate your concern, Sally,' she went on with a softening of her voice, genuinely fond of the other woman, despite the penchant she had for gossiping. 'But I can assure you I do know what I'm doing.'

How could she not know? Patrick had made it more than obvious that, while they would have a full marriage, and hopefully several children, love would never come into it.

That was what bothered her about this marriage. She was falling in love with a man who had told her quite bluntly he would never feel the same way about her. Courtesy of Sanchia. Well, he might have loved her very much, but the collapse of that marriage, in the way that it had, meant he would never love again. Legacy of Sanchia.

Lilli hated Patrick's first wife, and she had never even met her!

And how was she going to survive in a marriage without love, loving her husband, but never being loved by him in return?

Somehow this was worse than the completely loveless marriage she had initially anticipated.

So very much worse!

So, yes, she knew what she was doing, but she had no choice in the matter; the wedding was mere minutes away now instead of days—days that had flown by all too swiftly!—and, more importantly, her father's lawyers had already started work on bringing a case against Andy. In fact, he might already be aware of it!

Sally sat down, leaning forward conspiratorially. 'Well, Patrick is an absolutely—'

'Gorgeous man,' Lilli finished for her, smiling teasingly. 'I never realised before, Sally, the fascination you have for gorgeous men!' She stood up to pick up her veil, placing the circle of flowers on top of her shining hair, studying her reflection in the mirror. The 'sacrificial lamb' was well and truly ready for the altar!

'You're referring to your father, of course.' Sally ruefully accepted her teasing. 'I still can't believe he's the man from the party. When I arrived here the other day to find the two of you together in the sitting-room, I must admit that my first thought was you were being unfaithful to Patrick even before the wedding!' She gave a grimace. 'Do you think he's serious about Gerry? Or do I actually stand a chance where he's concerned?' She looked questioningly at Lilli.

'He isn't serious about Gerry,' Lilli replied defensively, her eyes flashing deeply green at the mere suggestion of it.

'So would you mind if I—?'

'Be my guest,' she invited, although the fact that her own father suddenly seemed very sought after, by beau-

tiful young women, was still a rather strange concept for
her to accept. Admittedly, he was only in his mid-forties,
but she had somehow never thought of him in that light
before. 'But for the record, Sally,' she went on, 'I don't
intend ever to be unfaithful to Patrick—before or after
the wedding!'

'Fine,' Sally accepted, grimacing at Lilli's vehemence.

'Sally…' Lilli remonstrated firmly.

Her friend held her hands up defensively. 'I believe
you—okay?'

Lilli laughed. 'Time will tell. In the meantime, I think
we have a wedding to go to!'

'Oh, gosh, yes.' Sally stood up hurriedly. 'It may be
traditional for the bride to be late, but in this case I'm
not so sure the groom wouldn't come looking for you!
I'll get off now, and see you at the registry office.' She
gave Lilli a reassuring hug before leaving.

Amazingly Lilli's conversation with Sally had lifted
her feelings somewhat, and she was smiling as she de-
scended the wide staircase, her smile widening warmly
as she saw her father standing at the bottom waiting for
her, looking especially handsome today in his grey
morning suit.

'Daddy, you look magnificent,' she praised glowingly
as she reached him.

'*I* look—!' There were tears in his eyes as he looked
down at her. 'Lilli, you look beautiful. So like your
mother did at this age. I wish she could have been here
to see you—'

'Not now, Daddy,' she dismissed briskly; talking
about her mother was the one thing she couldn't cope
with today, of all days. It was going to be difficult
enough to get through anyway, without thoughts of her

mother. Besides, she very much doubted this marriage was what her mother would have wished for her. It wouldn't do to dwell on that thought... 'Patrick will be becoming impatient,' she said brightly.

'Talking of Patrick...' Her father frowned, turning to the table that stood in the centre of the reception area, picking up a flat blue velvet box. 'He sent this for you earlier.' Her father snapped open the lid of the box, the two of them gasping as he revealed the most amazing necklace Lilli had ever seen. The emerald and diamond droplet in the centre of the delicate gold chain was an exact match for the engagement ring Lilli had transferred to her right hand for the marriage ceremony...

Her hand trembled slightly as she picked up the card that lay in the circle of gold, recognising the large scrawling handwriting as Patrick's before she even read the words written there. His cryptic sense of humour was all too apparent in the message.

Something new, Lilli—and if your eyes had been blue instead of green it could have been something blue too! Please wear it for me today.

Yours, Patrick.

'Lilli...!' her father breathed dazedly, still staring at the perfection of the necklace.

She swallowed hard, carefully replacing the card in the box before releasing the necklace and holding it out to her father. 'Would you help me put it on, Daddy?' She turned around, carefully lifting up her hair so that he could secure the catch. 'We'll have to hurry, Daddy,' she encouraged as he made no effort to do so. 'The car is waiting outside.'

'I still can't believe—Lilli, you're my little girl, and—'

'Please, Daddy.' Her own voice quivered with emotion. 'Put the necklace on and let's just go!' Before she totally destroyed the work of the last hour and began to cry.

He did so with slightly shaking fingers, careful not to ruffle her hair. 'Absolutely incredible,' her father said huskily as he stepped back to look at her.

Lilli gave a tight smile, not bothering to glance in the hall mirror as they walked out to the car. 'Only the best for Patrick. He would hardly give his future wife anything less.'

'I was referring to you, not the necklace,' her father gently rebuked. 'But then, you are the best; those jewels only enhance what is already perfection.'

She laughed. 'I think you may be slightly biased, Daddy!'

'I think Patrick Devlin is a very lucky man,' he stated. 'Take a deep breath before we go outside, Lilli,' he warned as he held her arm. 'I think half the world's press is gathered outside to snap a photograph of Patrick Devlin's bride!'

Which certainly wasn't an understatement!

A barrage of flashing cameras and intrusive microphones were pointed at the two of them as soon as they stepped outside into what was a crisply cold but bright, sunny December day. Questions were flung at them thick and fast, questions Lilli chose to ignore as she and her father hurried to the waiting car. The press had been hounding her continuously since the announcement of the wedding had appeared in the newspaper, and the wedding day itself had been sure to engender this excess of interest.

It was all so ridiculous to Lilli. Didn't these people have a war or something to write about and fill their newspapers with? This interest in what was, after all, just another society wedding, albeit with one of the principal players possibly being one of the richest men in England, seemed rather obscene to Lilli, and—

She was half in the car and half out of it when, her face paling, she caught sight of a familiar face amongst the crowd.

Andy...

She shook her head in denial of her imaginings. It couldn't have been Andy. Not here; this was the last place he would ever be seen. The only place she *wanted* to see him was in a courtroom, in the dock!

'Lilli...? Her father was waiting to get into the car beside her. 'What is it?' He saw her ashen cheeks.

'Nothing.' She turned to give him a glowing smile, the cameras clicking anew at what she supposed must look like the blushing bride on her way to her wedding. 'We'll be late if we don't go now,' she encouraged.

Her father looked as if he was about to add something to that, but at her determined expression he seemed to change his mind.

She had made her decision last week; there would be no last-minute nerves, no change of plan. That glimpse of someone she had thought looked a little like Andy had shaken her a little, but that was all...

'If I don't have the chance to tell you so again, you look absolutely beautiful,' Patrick whispered to her as they awaited the arrival of their guests to the private reception her father had organised at the Bennett Hotel.

Lilli barely glanced at him. She was almost afraid to. Half an hour ago she had married this man, was now

his wife—and she had never been so scared of anything
in her life before! In fact, she couldn't ever remember
feeling scared before at all.

But Patrick had seemed like a remote stranger when
they'd met at the registry office, making Lilli all too
aware that that was exactly what he was!

Brides who had known their groom for years, and
were secure in mutually expressed love, still had wed-
ding-day nerves over the rightness of what they were
doing; how much deeper, in the circumstances, was her
own trepidation?

Just looking at the man who was now her husband
was part of her panic. How on earth had she ever thought
she could spend the rest of her life with this man? He
was as good-looking as the devil, cool as ice, didn't love
her, and had assured her he never would. God, this
was—

'Gerry, when our guests arrive, greet them for us and
assure them we will be with them shortly.' Patrick spoke
quietly to his sister even as he grasped Lilli's arm.

Lilli's father frowned at him; the four of them had
been the first to arrive at the reception room. 'Where are
the two of you going?'

Patrick's hand was firm on Lilli's elbow as he led her
away. 'Upstairs to our suite so that I can kiss my bride
in private,' he told the other man grimly.

'But—'

'Let them go, Richard,' Gerry advised, her hand resting gently on his arm.

Lilli was shaking so badly now she could barely walk,
the thought of actually being alone with Patrick sending
her into a complete panic. This was real. Far, far too
real, as the warmth of Patrick's guiding hand on her arm
told her all too forcefully. It had seemed such a simple

decision to make—the only decision she could make in the circumstances!—but the reality of it was all too much. She wanted to scream. Run away. To shout—

'Not here,' Patrick said suddenly, moving swiftly to swing her up into his arms.

Much to the interest of all the other hotel guests who stood watching them, he strode purposefully through the lobby to the lifts, several indulgent smiles directed their way as people observed their hurried departure. It didn't need two guesses to know what these people were thinking. But they were wrong! So very wrong...

Patrick, literally kicked open the door to the suite he had arranged for them to stay in tonight, setting Lilli down once they were safely inside. She looked up at him with widely apprehensive eyes.

'*Now* you can scream,' he encouraged indulgently.

Her breath left her with a shaky sigh. 'It was that obvious?'

'Only to me,' he assured her. 'I'm only surprised this didn't happen earlier. You've been too controlled this last week—'

'But I am controlled.' She swung impatiently away from him, angry with herself because she didn't seem able to stop shaking. 'I'm just being very stupid now,' she confessed self-disgustedly.

'You're being a twenty-one-year-old young lady who just made probably the biggest decision of her entire life.' Patrick's hands gently squeezed her shoulders as he turned her to face him. 'But I promise you I'll treat you well. That I'll try to curb this urge I have to dominate. I will honour and cherish you,' he added gruffly.

But he wouldn't love her; that omission was all too apparent to Lilli.

'But it isn't that, is it…?' Patrick said slowly, studying her closely. 'Tell me what it is, Lilli?'

She couldn't possibly tell him how she felt, that as she'd looked at him earlier as they'd made their wedding vows to each other she had known that she, at least, meant every word. She wasn't falling in love with him— she had already done so!

There was absolutely no doubt in her mind that she loved Patrick. It was nothing like what she had felt for Andy, was so much more intense, so— Oh, God, Andy… Had it been him she had seen earlier, or just someone that looked very like him?

Patrick shook her gently as she frowned. 'What is it, Lilli?' There was an edge of urgency to his voice now.

'I thought— You're going to think I'm imagining things now. But I—I thought I saw Andy outside the house earlier.' She frowned again up at Patrick as he released her abruptly, his expression serious now. 'I told you it was stupid—'

'Not at all,' Patrick barked. 'I have it on good authority that Brewster is back in London.'

She swallowed hard. 'He is?' She suddenly felt very sick. After what Andy had done to her father, and to her, she had no wish for him ever to come near her again. But with Patrick's confirmation that he was in London she was even more convinced that it had been Andy she'd seen outside the house…

Why? What had he been doing there? What had he hoped to achieve by being outside her father's house on her wedding day to another man?

'It's a little late for second thoughts, Lilli.' Patrick was watching her closely. 'You're my wife now.'

With all that entailed. He owned her now; it was there in every arrogant inch of his tensely held body. Minutes ago, his gentleness and understanding drawing her close to him, she had almost been tempted to tell him how stupid she had been, that she was in love with him! Thank God she hadn't. She was a Devlin possession, a beautiful trophy to display on his arm, a wife with none of the complications of love involved.

She nodded in cool agreement. 'Our guests will have arrived downstairs.'

'You feel up to meeting them now?'

'Don't worry, Patrick, I won't embarrass you. My nerves simply got the better of me for a moment. It won't happen again.'

'No,' Patrick finally said slowly. 'I don't believe it will.'

Regret…? Or perhaps she had just imagined that particular emotion in his voice; the last thing he wanted was an emotional child for a wife. Her loss of control wouldn't happen again. After all, he had just assured her he would treat her well! He couldn't possibly realise that, loving him as she did, there were cruel things he could do to her…

And he must never know!

'We made a bargain, Patrick,' she told him distantly. 'And, like you, I never break my word once it's given.'

His expression hardened. 'I'm glad to hear it. Now, as you've already pointed out, our guests will be waiting.' He indicated she should precede him out of the suite, walking this time; the two of them were physically apart as well as emotionally.

That moment of gentleness and understanding was well and truly over, and for the next three hours Lilli didn't have the time even to think, concentrating on their guests, portraying the image that she and Patrick were a golden couple. There was no doubting they succeeded;

family and friends smiled at them indulgently every time
Lilli glanced around the large table where they all sat
eating their meal. No doubt the few members of her
family present thought she was very fortunate to have
married someone as eligible as Patrick, especially after
the 'Andy incident', as most of them referred to her previous engagement. Once the embezzlement story hit the
headlines, perhaps some of them would draw their own
conclusions, but for the moment everyone was obviously
enjoying themselves.

Except, Lilli noticed, the late arrival standing in the
doorway looking at the gathering with contemptuous
blue eyes...

She didn't recognise the woman, so she could only
assume she was a guest of Patrick's. A very beautiful
guest, Lilli acknowledged with a stab of jealousy. Tall
and blonde, with ice-blue eyes, she stood almost six feet
tall, with the slender elegance of a model about to make
an entrance onto the catwalk.

That icy blue gaze met Lilli's puzzled one, the
woman's red pouting mouth twisting contemptuously as
her hard eyes swept critically over Lilli—and obviously
found her wanting—before passing on to Patrick. Now
the blue eyes weren't so icy; in fact, they became posi-
tively heated, seeming to devour him at a glance!

Lilli felt herself bridle indignantly. How dared this
woman—whoever she was—come here and look at her
husband in that way? Patrick had told her, several times,
that there had been no women in his life since his marriage ended, but the way this woman was looking at him
seemed to tell a very different story!

Lilli's indignation rose. If she belonged to Patrick
now, then he also belonged to her, and women from his
past had no place at their wedding reception.

She turned to him sharply. 'Patrick—'

'My God...!' he exclaimed even as she spoke, the intensity of the blonde woman's stare somehow seeming to have made him aware of her presence in the doorway, his face set grimly, a nerve pulsing in his jaw. 'What the hell...?' he ground out disbelievingly.

Lilli blinked at him, unsure of his mood. She had seen him mocking, contemptuous, coldly angry, passionately aroused, even gently teasing, but she had no idea what emotion he was feeling as he took in the woman in the doorway. Every muscle in his body seemed to be tensed, and his fingers looked in danger of snapping the slender stem of the champagne glass he held.

'Patrick...?' Lilli prompted uncertainly now.

His glass landed with a thump on the table-top as he stood up abruptly, unseeing as he looked down at her. 'I'll be back in a few minutes,' he grated, turning to leave.

Lilli didn't need to be told he was going to the woman across the room, a woman he obviously knew very well if that blaze of awareness in the woman's eyes as she looked at him had been anything to go by! He couldn't do this to her, not at their wedding reception!

'Let him go, Lilli,' his sister advised quietly as Lilli would have reached out and stopped his departure. Gerry was looking across the room at the blond woman too now.

Lilli's mouth tightened resentfully, both at Gerry's intervention and Patrick's powerful strides across the room towards the beautiful woman. Her eyes flashed deeply green as she turned to the woman who was now her sister-in-law. 'You know that woman?' she asked.

'Oh, yes.' Gerry's mouth twisted contemptuously, although her gaze was soft as she looked at Lilli. 'I'm hardly likely to forget the woman who made Patrick into the hardened cynic he is today!'

Sanchia!

The beautiful woman in the doorway, the woman who had looked at Patrick so possessively, was his ex-wife? Here? Now?

Lilli turned sharply, just in time to see Sanchia smile seductively up at Patrick, before he took a firm hold of her arm and forcefully escorted her from the room.

CHAPTER NINE

'GERRY...? What the hell is she doing here?' Lilli's father hissed agitatedly.

Lilli turned to him. 'You know Patrick's ex-wife too?'

'Of course. Your mother and I were part of that crowd five years ago,' he reminded her.

Before her mother's illness became such that it was impossible for her to go anywhere...

'Where are you going, Lilli?' Her father's hand on her arm restrained her as she stood up.

Her expression was calm, a smile curving her lips— even if the green of her eyes spat fire. 'I'm going to join my bridegroom,' she told him, releasing her arm. 'Don't worry, Daddy.' Her smile was wry now at his expression of panic. 'I can assure you, I intend it to be a civilised meeting.'

Gerry grimaced. 'Sanchia isn't known for her civility!'

Lilli gave a genuinely warm smile as she bent down to answer the other woman. 'I'll let you into a secret, Gerry,' she murmured. 'Neither am I when I'm pushed into a corner!' She straightened, looking towards the door through which Patrick had left so hastily minutes earlier. 'And I've just been pushed,' she muttered as she turned to move determinedly towards that door.

Gerry touched her arm lightly as she passed her. 'Just watch out for the claws,' she warned.

Lilli nodded her thanks. 'I'll do that.'

It wasn't difficult to locate Patrick and Sanchia once

she was out in the corridor; the sound of raised voices came from a room a little further down the hallway, Patrick's icily calm, the female voice—Sanchia's—raised to the point of hysteria.

The claws Gerry had warned Lilli about were raised in the direction of Patrick's face as Lilli silently entered the room, Patrick's hands on the other woman's wrists to prevent her nails actually making contact with his cheeks.

'Dear, dear, dear,' Lilli murmured mockingly as she closed the door firmly behind her. 'Do I take it this isn't a happy reunion?'

The two people already in the room were frozen as if in a tableau. Both turned to face Lilli as she calmly stood looking at them, dark brows raised questioningly. Patrick looked far from pleased at the interruption, but Sanchia slowly lowered her hands, her icy blue eyes suddenly speculative as she looked Lilli up and down.

'The bride,' she drawled derisively.

Lilli steadily met the other woman's contemptuous glare. 'And the ex-bride,' she returned just as scathingly, knowing she had scored a direct hit as Sanchia's mouth tightened furiously. 'Patrick, our guests are waiting,' Lilli reminded him lightly.

Sanchia released her arms from Patrick's steely grip, eyes blazing. 'Unless he's changed a great deal—which I very much doubt!—Patrick doesn't respond well to orders!' The accent to her English was slightly more noticeable in this longer speech.

Green eyes met icy blue. 'Patrick hasn't changed. In any way,' Lilli added pointedly. 'Darling?' she prompted again.

He couldn't let her down now. He just couldn't! If he did, their marriage was over before it had even begun.

No matter what his feelings towards Sanchia—and Lilli really had no idea what they were, or indeed about the other woman's towards him; Sanchia had obviously felt strongly enough about something, possibly Patrick, to have turned up here today!—it was Lilli he was married to now. And she had married him. For better or for worse.

To her relief Patrick walked determinedly to her side, his expression grim as his arm moved possessively about her waist. 'As I've told you, Sanchia—' he looked at his former wife resolutely '—there's no place for you here.'

'This—this child—' Sanchia looked at Lilli scornfully '—could never take my place in your life! You need a real woman, Patrick—and I was always that.'

Lilli stiffened at this mention of intimacy between the two, although her outward expression remained calm. She didn't particularly want to hear about Patrick's marriage to Sanchia. And Patrick, his arm still about her waist, must have felt her reaction.

'Patrick likes them a little younger nowadays,' Lilli told Sanchia wryly, knowing by the angry flush that appeared in the other woman's cheeks that her barb had hit its mark. Sanchia was probably only ten years older than her, but she obviously felt those years...

'Inexperienced, you mean,' Sanchia returned bitchily. 'Patrick bores easily too,' she warned.

Lilli smiled. 'I'm sure you would know that better than I.' She felt the tightening of Patrick's hand on her waist, but chose to ignore it; she knew she was playing with fire, but at this particular moment she didn't mind getting her fingers burnt.

Sanchia gave a snort before turning to Patrick. 'I give this marriage a matter of months, darling,' she drawled, picking her bag up from the table. 'And I'll still be around when it's over. In fact, I'm thinking of moving to New York.'

'Really? I'm sure you'll enjoy the life over there.' Patrick was the one to answer her. 'Frankly—' his arm settled more comfortably about Lilli's waist '—I'm tired of it. Lilli and I will be living in London.'

That was news to Lilli! They hadn't so much as mentioned where they would live after their marriage since the night Patrick had given her the engagement ring, and she had behaved so stupidly about moving to New York. Now, it seemed, they weren't going to live there at all...

'I don't believe it,' Sanchia gasped. 'You've always loved New York.'

He gave an acknowledging nod. 'And now I love Lilli—and her family and friends are all in London.'

Two bright spots of angry colour appeared in Sanchia's cheeks. 'My family and friends were in Paris, but you refused to live there!' she accused heatedly, turning to Lilli with furious blue eyes. 'Enjoy his indulgence while you can,' she advised. 'I can assure you, it doesn't last for long!'

Considering one of this woman's indulgences had been other men, that wasn't so surprising!

Lilli met her gaze unflinchingly. 'I wouldn't hold your breath,' she said.

Sanchia gave a hard smile. 'Or you yours! Take care, Patrick.' She reached out to run a caressing hand down his cheek lightly. 'And remember, I'm still here.'

This last, Lilli knew, was said for her benefit. And while a visit from an ex-wife was enough to chill the heart of any new one—no matter what the circumstances of the divorce had been, the previous wife having an intimate knowledge of the man, of his likes and dislikes, that was totally intrusive—at that moment Lilli didn't feel in the least threatened by the other woman, had seen the look of absolute loathing in Patrick's face for Sanchia when she'd entered this room a few minutes ago. Patrick disliked his ex-wife intensely.

'Excuse us,' Patrick told Sanchia coldly. 'We have a wedding reception to attend.' His hand was firm against Lilli's back as he guided her to the door, neither of them looking back as they left. '"Patrick likes them younger nowadays"?' he repeated as soon as the two of them were out of earshot in the hallway.

Lilli glanced up at him from beneath lowered lashes, knowing by the curve to his mouth that he wasn't in the least angry at her remark. 'I believe I said "a *little* younger",' she returned, grinning up at him mischievously.

Patrick looked down at her, shaking his head incredulously. 'You weren't in the least thrown by her appearance here, were you?'

She wouldn't go quite so far as to say that, but if it was what Patrick believed...

She shrugged, the two of them standing outside the reception room now. 'Should I have been?'

'Not at all,' he returned easily. 'The part of my life that contained Sanchia is dead and buried as far as I'm concerned.' His expression was grim.

'That's what I thought.' Lilli accepted—gratefully, inside!—putting her hand in the crook of his arm. 'Let's join our guests; you still have a speech to give!'

'Oh, God, yes,' he groaned. 'I'm not quite sure what to say about my bride any more,' he added dryly.

Lilli grinned. 'Beautiful. Intelligent. Undemanding—'

'Sometimes wise beyond her years,' he put in. 'And full of surprises. I was sure you would give me hell over

Sanchia turning up here, today of all days. Full of surprises...'

She shook her head. 'You can't be held responsible for the actions of a vindictive woman. She wanted to cause trouble between us, unnerve you, and upset me— I vote we don't give her the satisfaction!'

'I stopped caring years ago about anything that Sanchia does,' Patrick revealed. 'I was more worried about you and how you would feel about it.'

And she could see that he had been, his concern still in the deep grey of his eyes. 'Don't be,' she told him brightly, needing no further assurances from him concerning his ex-wife. 'And as for being full of surprises— when did *we* decide to live in London?' She quirked dark brows again.

He frowned in thought. 'I believe it was the night we became engaged.'

'No.' Lilli shook her head. 'You refused to even discuss it then.'

'Because at the time I was intent on kissing you, if I remember correctly.' He grinned as she blushed at the memory. 'But your wish not to live in New York was duly noted, and—'

'Acted upon.' Lilli frowned. 'I can see I'll have to be more careful about what I say in future. Or was Sanchia right about your indulgence?' she added teasingly. 'Won't it last?'

Patrick's arms moved smoothly about her waist. 'It isn't a question of indulging you, Lilli. You said you didn't want to live in New York, and, as I have no feelings either way, it seems obvious that we live here. I want you to be happy in our marriage,' he added gruffly. 'And if living in London is going to help do that, then this is where we'll live. I thought, with your agreement, that we could go house-hunting in the new year?'

He probably couldn't see it—and, in the circumstances, Lilli had no intention of pointing it out to him, either, because living in London suited her fine!—but the fact that he had made this decision on his own, without any consultation with her, was an act of arrogance in itself.

'Fine,' she nodded.

'Do you mind staying here in the hotel until we find a house? I somehow don't think we should move in with either your father or my sister.'

Lilli grimaced. 'Certainly not!'

Patrick grinned. 'Ditto.'

She blinked up at him. 'That's amazing, Patrick; do you realise that's three things we've agreed on in the last five minutes?'

'Three things...?' He looked serious as he thought back over their conversation.

She nodded. 'To live in London. And that your ex-wife is a bitch! She even chose to wear a white suit to come here today.' Lilli had duly noted the deliberate ploy of Sanchia to upstage the bride; the beautiful silk suit obviously had a designer label, and white was usually the colour reserved for the bride on her wedding day. She didn't doubt that Sanchia had been reminding her that she had been Patrick's bride first!

He grimaced. 'But the jacket, if I remember correctly, was edged with black. And Sanchia is more black than white!'

There was so much pain behind that stark comment. Lilli could only hope that one day he would feel comfortable enough in their relationship to talk to her about the marriage that had ended so disastrously.

For the first time that she could remember in their acquaintance Lilli was the one to reach up and initiate a kiss between them.

Patrick seemed as surprised as she was to start with, and then he kissed her back.

It hadn't been premeditated on her part; Lilli could have had no idea Sanchia would choose that particular moment to storm out of the reception room further down the hallway. But that was exactly what she did, her eyes narrowing glacially as she took in the scene of intimacy. With one last furious glare in their direction, she turned on her heel and walked away.

For good, Lilli hoped.

'Good timing,' Patrick told her dryly as he grasped her elbow to take her back to their guests.

He believed she had kissed him at that moment deliberately, so that Sanchia would see them!

And perhaps it was better if he continued to think that, Lilli decided as they moved around the huge dining-room chatting to each of their guests. Patrick had clearly stated he did not want a wife who loved him, only one that would be faithful and loyal.

Loving him as she did, those two things would be quite easy to be, and it was best to leave it at that...

'Thank goodness that's over!' Patrick pulled off his bow-tie with some relief, discarding his jacket onto a chair too, unbuttoning the top button of his shirt. 'I thought your father and Gerry were never going to leave.'

Lilli smiled at the memory of her father dithering about downstairs, drinking two glasses of champagne that he really didn't want, simply because now the time had come for him to leave Lilli alone with her husband and he was reluctant to do so.

She shook her head. 'And I thought the bride was the one that was nervous; you would have thought it was Daddy's wedding night the way he kept so obviously delaying our departure upstairs!' She smiled affectionately, sitting in one of the armchairs in the sitting-room of their suite, her veil discarded hours ago, the tea-roses still entwined in the flowing darkness of her hair.

Patrick looked across at her with dark grey eyes. 'And are you?' he said gruffly. 'Nervous,' he explained softly at her frown.

She swallowed hard. 'A little,' she acknowledged huskily.

He came down on his haunches beside her chair. 'You don't have to be, you know.' He smoothed the hair back from her cheeks. 'It's been a pretty eventful day, one way or another. And now it's very late, and we're both tired, and we have the rest of our lives together. I suggest we both take a shower and then get some sleep.' He straightened. 'There are two bathrooms in this suite; you take one and I'll take the other.'

Lilli looked at him dazedly as he picked up his jacket. He didn't want her!

'Lilli?'

She focused on him with effort. He was so tall and masculine, so devastatingly attractive. And he was her husband.

Damn it, she wanted to make love with him! This was their wedding night. And a part of her—the part that wasn't nervous!—had been anticipating the two of them making love. And now he had decided they weren't going to, after all...

He gave an impatient sigh. 'Stop looking at me as if

I've just hit you! I'm not a monster, Lilli, and I can see
how tired you are. A shower and then sleep will be the
best thing for you at the moment.'

The exhaustion she had felt on their way up here had
suddenly vanished. Patrick didn't want to make love to
her! Was this the way it was when you didn't marry for
love? Or was he more affected by Sanchia's visit than
he had admitted? Had seeing the other woman again
made him realise he had made a mistake? What—?

'You're letting your imagination run away with you
now,' he rasped suddenly, looking at her assessingly.
'Asking yourself questions that, in the clear light of day,
you will recognise as nonsensical. I'm trying to be a
gentleman, Lilli,' he explained. 'But if it makes you feel
better I could always throw you down on the carpet right
now and—'

'No!' she cut in forcefully, getting to her feet, avoiding looking at him as she did so. 'I'll go and take that
shower.'

He nodded abruptly. 'I'll see you shortly.'

Lilli went through to the bedroom; her clothes had
been brought here the day before and unpacked into the
drawers. She took out the white silk nightgown before
going through to the adjoining bathroom, thankfully
closing the door behind her.

She had made a fool of herself just now, and it wasn't
a feeling she was comfortable with. Patrick wasn't an
eager bridegroom, in love with his new wife, desperate
to make love with her. There was no urgency to con-
summate their marriage. They had plenty of time for
that...

Patrick was already in bed when she came through
from the bathroom half an hour later, the sheet resting
about his waist, his chest bare, the hair there dark and

curling, his skin lightly tanned. His hair was still damp from his shower, and he looked—

Lilli quickly looked away as he turned towards her, knowing the flare of desire she felt at the sight of him would be evident in her eyes. 'I'm sorry I took so long.' She moved about the room, hanging up her wedding dress and veil. 'It took me ages to get the flowers out of my hair and then pull a brush through it.' She held up a hand to her long vibrant hair. 'And then I—'

'Lilli, just leave all that and get into bed,' he interrupted wearily. 'You're wearing me out just watching you! It isn't as if it matters whether or not the dress gets creased; you won't be wearing it again.'

She thrust the dress on its hanger into the back of the wardrobe, as if it had burnt her. No, she wouldn't be wearing it again. Because she would always be married to Patrick. And look how disastrous it was turning out to be!

'Don't make me come and get you, Lilli,' Patrick urged as she still made no effort to get into the bed beside him. 'I never wear anything in bed, and I have a feeling you're the one that would end up feeling embarrassed if I were to get up right now!'

She scrambled into the bed beside him so quickly that her foot became entangled in the sheet and threatened to pull the damn thing off him anyway!

How stupidly she was behaving; she inwardly sighed once she had finally settled onto her own side of the wide double bed. Not at all like the normally composed Lilli. And as for Elizabeth Bennett...!

Patrick reached out to switch off the light, lying back in the darkness.

Lilli lay stiffly on her side of the bed, her eyes adjusting to the small amount of light shining into the room through the curtains at the window. She was never going to be able to sleep, couldn't possibly—

'If it's not too much to ask—' Patrick spoke softly beside her '—*I* would like to give my wife a cuddle before we go to sleep.'

She swallowed hard as he propped himself up on one elbow to look down at her, his individual features not discernible to her, although she could make out the shadows of his face. And he looked as if he was smiling!

'*Is* it too much to ask?' he prompted huskily.

'Of course not.' She moved in the darkness, putting her head on his shoulder as he lay back against the pillow, his arm curved around her, his hand resting possessively on her hip, the warmth of his body—his naked body!—instantly warming her too.

He gave a sigh of contentment, turning to kiss her temple lightly. 'This is worth all of the hectic circus today has been.' He relaxed against her.

Lilli still felt unsure of herself. Through the ridiculousness of his marriage proposal, her reluctant acceptance of it, the hectic activity during the week that followed, she had never doubted that Patrick desired her. In fact, he had seemed to have great difficulty keeping his hands off her! But now they were married, alone together at last, he didn't seem—

'You're letting your imagination run away with you again. Lilli, has it ever occurred to you that maybe *I'm* a little nervous?'

'You?' She turned to him, raising her head in surprise.

'Yes. Me,' he confirmed, pushing her head back down onto his shoulder. 'I told you, it's a long time since I did this. Maybe I've forgotten how to do it. Maybe I won't be able to please you.' He gave a deep sigh. 'God knows, the last time I attempted to make love to a woman, she fell asleep before we even got started! I'm talking about *you*, Lilli,' he explained as he felt her stiffen defensively in his arms. 'Five minutes earlier you had been full of sensual promise, and then—nothing.'

She buried her face in his shoulder at the memory. 'I had too much to drink. It had nothing to do with—with—'

'Well, it did absolutely nothing for my ego,' he assured her. 'Now will you accept that and just leave this for tonight?'

When he put it that way—of course she would! She had never imagined that Patrick had moments of uncertainty too. He was so damned arrogant most of the time, it was difficult to imagine him being nervous about anything. Certainly not about making love to her!

'Of course I will.' She snuggled closer to him in the darkness, her hand resting lightly on his chest. 'Mm, this is nice,' she murmured contentedly.

'Go to sleep, Lilli,' he muttered.

She slept. Not because Patrick had ordered her to, but because, as he'd said, she was truly exhausted.

Quite what woke her she had no idea, but as she slowly came awake she realised it was probably because she had subconsciously registered that she was alone in the bed, the lean length of Patrick no longer beside her.

She looked sleepily around the bedroom, realising by the fact that it was still dark in the room that it must be quite early. She finally located Patrick sitting in the chair by the window, a dark robe pulled on over his nakedness.

She moved up onto her elbows, blinking sleepily across at him. 'Patrick...?'

'Who the hell is Robbie?' he returned harshly.

CHAPTER TEN

LILLIE was dazed, not really awake yet, totally thrown by the savagely accusing question.

Patrick surged forcefully to his feet, crossing the room to sit down on the side of the bed, instantly tightening the bedclothes above her, holding her pinned to the mattress. He placed his hands on the pillow at either side of her head, glaring down at her in the semi-darkness. 'I want to know who Robbie is,' he repeated in a harsh, controlled voice.

Lilli pushed her tousled hair back from her forehead. 'I don't— What—?'

'Imagine my surprise,' Patrick ground out, 'when my bride of a few hours starts calling for another man—a man I've never heard of!—in her sleep!'

She swallowed hard, moistening her lips. She didn't remember dreaming at all, certainly not of Robbie. But Patrick said she had called out his name...? 'I did that?' She frowned her confusion.

Patrick's mouth twisted. 'It's hardly something I'm likely to have made up, is it?' he grated.

No, of course it wasn't. She just couldn't imagine why she had done such a thing...

'Lilli, I'm not going to ask you again.' He grasped her shoulders. 'Who the hell is he?'

She turned away from the livid anger in his face. '*Was* he,' she corrected him chokily. 'He's dead.'

Patrick released her abruptly, sitting back now, no

longer leaning over her so oppressively. 'You loved him,' he stated flatly.

'Very much,' she confirmed shakily.

He stood up to pace the room. 'I don't believe this! Now I have a damned ghost to contend with as well as an ex-fiancé...!' He shook his head disgustedly. 'No one has ever mentioned someone in your life called Robbie.' He glared at her.

'There was no need for them to do so,' she said heavily, painful memories assailing her anew. 'He's been dead a long time.' She sighed. 'Patrick, Robbie was—'

'I can guess,' he cut in savagely. 'He was the reason you settled for someone like Andy Brewster. The reason you're now married to me. He was—'

'The person that gave me the name Lilli,' she told him, her voice very small. 'Remember you once asked me about my name? Actually, it was Lillibet originally,' she recalled sadly. 'But over the years it's been short-ened to Lilli.'

'Lillibet?' Patrick repeated. 'It sounds like something a child might say. What sort of—?'

'It *was* something a child might say—a very young child,' she told him slowly, no longer looking at him, her vision all inwards, on the past, on memories of Robbie. 'Robbie couldn't get his tongue around the name Elizabeth, and so his version came out as Lillibet.' She smiled at the memory, that smile fading as quickly as it appeared. 'He was only two when he died of men-ingitis.' She looked at Patrick with dull eyes. 'He was my brother.'

Patrick paled. 'He— But— I—'

Patrick at a loss for words would have been funny

under any other circumstances. But at the moment it was lost on her.

'I was eleven when he died. One day he was here, giggling and fun, and the next he had— I—I—' She fought the control she always lost when talking of her brother. 'I loved him from the day he was born. Perhaps the difference in our ages helped with that; I don't know.' She shook her head. 'But I could never accept— I didn't understand. In some ways I still don't. He was beautiful.' She looked at Patrick with tear-wet eyes. 'I loved him so much,' she added brokenly. 'I have no idea why I called for him last night. I don't remember. I just—'

'Hey, it's all right.' Patrick sank down beside her on the bed, his arms moving about her as he held her close against him. 'I had no idea, Lilli. I'm so sorry. I do vaguely remember something—God, I'm just making this worse.' He angrily berated himself. 'I shouldn't "vaguely remember" anything! Robbie was your brother—'

'But you didn't know him. You didn't know us.' Her voice was muffled against his chest. 'Robbie was special to me; I still can't think of him without crying. I'm sorry.' She began to cry in earnest now.

'Lilli, please don't cry,' Patrick groaned. 'I do know what it's like to lose someone you love. I was seven when my mother gave birth to Gerry. Gerry was born, and my mother died. I was left with that same bewilderment you obviously were. And my father and I were left with the onerous task of bringing up a new-born baby. For fifteen years we managed to do exactly that, and then my father died, and it was left completely to me.'

As he spoke of his mother and father, his childhood

with Gerry, his voice somehow lost its smoothness, acquiring a slightly Irish lilt to it. And Lilli could only guess, from the emotion in his voice, just how difficult it had been for him to lose his mother—and be presented with a totally helpless baby.

His statements had been starkly made, telling her about none of the trauma he and his father must have felt in surviving such sorrow. Or how difficult it must have been for him, at only twenty-two, to have the sole charge of a fifteen-year-old girl. And yet he had done it and, from the success he had made of his business life and the closeness between himself and Gerry, all too capably.

Lilli shook her head. 'I didn't know—'

'Why should you?' He lightly touched her hair. 'We have the rest of our lives to get to know about each other, both past and present.'

Lilli hoped that would include speaking about his marriage to Sanchia. As she looked up into the gentleness of his face, she thought it would...

'I didn't mean to make you cry just now,' he continued. 'I only—I just— I was jealous,' he admitted. 'I thought he was a man you had cared for.'

She looked up at him with puzzled, tear-wet eyes. If he had felt jealousy, did that mean he cared for her, after all? Even as her heart leapt at the thought, she realised it wasn't that at all; what Patrick possessed, he possessed exclusively. Didn't he despise Sanchia because she hadn't been exclusively his?

She shook her head. 'You need have no worries like that concerning me. Andy was my one and only venture into commitment—and look how disastrously that turned out!'

Patrick settled himself on the bed beside her. 'Well,

you're totally committed now,' he told her with satisfaction. 'How does it feel?'

'Not a lot different than before.'

He looked at her with teasing eyes. 'Do I detect a note of disappointment in your voice?'

Did he? Possibly. There couldn't be too many virgin brides who had built themselves up to being made love to on their wedding night—only to be told by their bridegroom that he was too tired! Although that wasn't strictly true... He had said they were both too tired. And the proof of her own tiredness was that she couldn't even remember falling asleep, although she must have done so almost immediately she shut her eyes.

But she wasn't sleepy now; in fact, she was wide awake... and suddenly very aware of Patrick as he lay beside her wearing only a robe to hide his nakedness.

Patrick gently raised her chin, smoky grey eyes looking straight into candid green. 'I know what you were thinking last night, Lilli,' he said gruffly. 'Oh, yes, I do,' he insisted as she would have protested. 'But the truth of the matter is, I want you too much, want us to enjoy each other too much, to have it spoilt in any way.'

She swallowed hard, the desire he spoke of evident in the burning intensity of his gaze. 'We're not tired now,' she pointed out shyly.

He laughed. 'No, we're not. And we are going to make love, Lilli.' He bent his head, his mouth claiming hers, lips moving erotically against hers, the tip of his tongue lightly caressing the inner moisture of her mouth.

Her arms curved up about his neck as she held him close to her, heart pounding, his hair feeling soft and silky beneath her fingertips, shoulders and back firmly muscled.

Lilli relaxed against the pillows, pulling Patrick with

her, his robe and her nightgown easily disposed of as flesh met flesh, Lilli's softness against Patrick's hardness, the dark hair on his chest tickling the sensitive tips of her breasts now.

And then Patrick's lips were teasing those sensitive tips, Lilli's head back as she gasped at the liquid fire that coursed through her body, groaning low in her throat as she felt the moist warmth of his tongue flicking over her hardened nipples.

His lips and hands caressed every part of her body during the timeless hours before dawn, encouraging her to touch him in return, to discover how he liked to be caressed too, to be kissed. But she seemed to know that instinctively, revelling in the response her lips and hands evoked, until his tender ministrations reached the most intimate part of her body and she could no longer think straight as heat such as she had never known before consumed her in flames.

And then Patrick was once more kissing her on the lips, his hands on her breasts as he slowly raised her to fulfilment once again. And again. And again.

And when his body finally joined with hers there was no pain, only pleasure of another kind, his slow, caressing movements deep inside her taking her to another plateau completely. A plateau Patrick joined her on, his own groans of pleasure merging with hers, before they lay damply together, their bodies merged, their breathing deep and ragged.

'I don't think you could have forgotten a thing,' Lilli finally said when she at last found the strength to talk.

Patrick laughed. 'I hope not—any more than that and I could die of a heart attack!'

She lay on top of him, moving slightly so that she could look into his face, unconcerned with her nakedness

now; there wasn't an inch of her body that Patrick didn't
now know intimately. 'You weren't nervous at all last
night, were you?' she realised shakily.

'You needed time to get used to me.'

'Used to' him; she was totally possessed by him at
this moment! 'But you weren't really nervous, were
you?' she persisted.

'Lilli.' He smoothed the tangled hair back over her
shoulders, revealing the pertness of her breasts. 'If you
only knew the ways I've imagined making love to you!'

He still hadn't answered her question. Or perhaps he
had... He had been thinking of her last night, giving her
time to become accustomed to their new relationship.

'I think I just experienced them,' she recalled breath-
lessly.

'Oh, no, Lilli. We've barely touched the surface,' he
assured her with promise.

She quivered in anticipation, only able to imagine the
delights yet to come.

'But not right now,' Patrick soothed, settling her head
comfortably against his shoulder. 'Now we're going to
have a nap.'

She swallowed hard. 'Like this?'

'Exactly like this,' he said with satisfaction. 'I like
having you as part of me. And vice versa, I hope.' He
quirked dark eyebrows.

'Oh, yes,' she admitted shyly, very much aware of the
way in which he was still 'part of' her! 'But it must be
late.' Daylight was visible now through the curtains at
the window. 'Shouldn't we—?'

'This is the morning after our wedding, Lilli,' he
teased. 'No one, least of all the hotel staff, will expect
to hear from us for hours yet. At which time we will
order breakfast—even if it's two o'clock in the after-

noon. This is a Bennett hotel; I'm sure they will accommodate us!'

Lilli was sure they would too. But whether or not she would ever, as the owner's daughter, be able to face any of the hotel staff again after her honeymoon was another matter!

But for the moment she didn't care, was content in Patrick's arms, being with him like this. And as she drifted off into sleep she had a feeling she always would be...

'What the hell—?'

Lilli woke suddenly, to the sound of Patrick's swearing, and the reason for it—a loud knocking on the outer door of their hotel suite.

She sat up groggily, just in time to see Patrick pulling on his robe and tying the belt tightly about his waist. 'I thought you said no one would disturb us today?' she giggled, pulling the sheet up to her chin as she watched him.

'I didn't think anyone would dare to!' He scowled darkly, glaring in the direction of the loud banging. 'It had better be for a good reason!'

As he strode out of the bedroom to the suite door Lilli couldn't help but feel sorry for the person who was standing on the other side of it, although she had to admit she was a little annoyed at the intrusion herself. Patrick's words, before they'd both fallen asleep, had promised so much more...

He didn't return immediately, as she had expected he would, and finally her lethargy turned to curiosity; it must be something important to keep Patrick away this long. She could hear the murmur of male voices in the sitting-room...

She pulled on her white silk robe over her nakedness, belting it securely before running a brush lightly through her hair; she might have just spent several hours of pleasure in her husband's arms, but she didn't want everyone to realise that just by looking at her!

'Daddy!' She gasped her surprise as she saw he was the man talking to Patrick. 'Good grief, Daddy, what on earth are you doing here?' She shook her head dazedly.

'Would you believe he came to make sure I hadn't strangled you on our wedding night?' Patrick drawled derisively. 'Or you hadn't stuck that knife in my back that he once suggested!'

Lilli looked at the two men, her father flushed and agitated, Patrick calm and controlled. 'Actually—no,' she answered firmly. 'So, why are you really here, Daddy?' she prompted.

'You certainly didn't raise a fool, Richard,' Patrick said appreciatively.

The older man gave him an exasperated glare before turning back to Lilli. 'Good afternoon, Lilli,' he greeted her. 'I'm sorry to interrupt—I mean, I realise I shouldn't have—' He broke off awkwardly, the way they were both dressed—or undressed!—telling its own story. 'Gerry told me I shouldn't come here...'

'You should have listened to her,' Patrick bit out tersely. 'I, for one, do not appreciate the interruption.'

Lilli had stilled at the mention of the other woman's name. Then she remembered how kind Gerry had been to her yesterday when Sanchia had appeared so inappropriately at the wedding. Although she still resented the other woman's place in her father's life, some of what Patrick had told her earlier about his sister made her realise that, as her own father was to her, Gerry was all the family Patrick had. And, as such, Lilli couldn't continue to alienate her.

'Perhaps you *should* have listened to her,' she told her father quietly.

Her father's eyes widened, but he didn't comment on the lack of the usual resentment in her voice when she spoke of the other woman. 'Maybe I should,' he agreed. 'But I thought this was important.'

Lilli returned his gaze frowningly; he must have done to risk Patrick's wrath by intruding on their honeymoon in this way. And he had obviously got more than he bargained for by finding them so obviously still in bed! 'How important?' she said slowly.

'Very,' he insisted firmly.

'I disagree,' Patrick put in hardly.

Lilli's father shot him a questioning glance. 'I think that's for Lilli to decide, don't you...?'

Patrick's head went back arrogantly. 'As it happens, no. I don't think this concerns Lilli at all. Not any more.'

She was intrigued by the mystery of her father's visit. Obviously, whatever it was about, Patrick didn't want her involved in it.

She moved to sit on one of the armchairs. 'Tell me,' she prompted her father.

He glanced uncertainly at the younger man, obviously far from reassured by Patrick's stony expression.

'Daddy!' Lilli encouraged impatiently.

He no longer met her gaze. 'Perhaps Patrick is right; this can wait until after your honeymoon—'

'We've had our honeymoon,' she assured him firmly. 'Have you forgotten we're joining you tomorrow for Christmas.' She didn't even look at Patrick now, knowing she would see disapproval in his face. But she was not a child, and she refused to be treated like one, by either man.

Her father slumped down into another of the armchairs. 'I'd completely forgotten it's Christmas…!' he groaned.

'Don't let Gerry hear you say that,' Patrick warned mockingly. 'She loves Christmas. I suggest you make sure you have something suitable for her by tomorrow!'

'Stop trying to change the subject, Patrick.' Again Lilli didn't so much as look at him. 'I'm not so easily deterred.'

'Does that mean you've already bought my Christmas present?' he returned tauntingly.

She had, as a matter of fact—a beautiful watch, already wrapped and ready to give him on Christmas morning. But that wasn't important just now.

'It means,' she said with slow determination, 'that I'm not going to be sidetracked. Daddy!' She was even more forceful this time.

'She gets her stubbornness from me, I'm afraid,' he told the younger man ruefully.

'It's irrelevant where she gets it from,' Patrick dismissed tersely. 'This is none of her business.'

'I'll be the judge of that,' she snapped. She had been kept in the dark too much already by these two men; it wasn't going to continue.

'You aren't Elizabeth Bennett any more, Lilli,' Patrick rasped. 'You're Mrs Lilli Devlin. And *Mr* Devlin has already decided this does not concern you!'

She stood up angrily. '*Mr* Devlin doesn't own me,' she returned furiously. 'Maybe someone should have told you: women aren't chattels any more! Now, either one of you tells me what's going on, or I'll go and ask someone who will tell me,' she added challengingly.

Patrick looked at her scathingly. 'Such as who?'

'Such as Gerry!' she announced triumphantly, knowing by the stunned look on both the men's faces that this hadn't even occurred to them as a possibility. Lilli wasn't so sure it was either; she might feel less antagonistic towards the other woman, but she wasn't sure she would be able to go to her about this! But hopefully neither of these two men would realise that... 'Well?' she prompted hardly when her announcement didn't produce the result she wanted, looking from one man to the other, her father looking decidedly uncomfortable, Patrick stubbornly unmoved. 'Fine,' she finally snapped, walking towards the bedroom, her clear intention to go and dress before leaving. 'Gerry it is!'

'Lilli, I forbid you to go anywhere near Gerry!' Patrick thundered autocratically.

She halted in her tracks, turning slowly, looking at him with cool incredulity.

'Uh-oh,' her father muttered warily. 'You've done it now, Patrick. The last time I forbade Lilli from going near someone she ended up *marrying* you!'

Patrick's mouth quirked. 'That hardly applies in this case, does it? Besides, it's because Lilli is married to me that I—'

'Think you can tell me what to do,' she finished scathingly, shaking her head. 'I don't think so,' she bit out coldly. 'Daddy?' she prompted in a voice that brooked no further argument.

He sighed, giving a regretful glance in Patrick's direction before turning back to Lilli. 'Andy telephoned me this morning,' he stated without flourish.

She gasped in shock. Whatever she had been expecting, it wasn't this!

She froze momentarily. 'Andy did...?'

Her father nodded. 'He wants to see you, Lilli,' he told her softly.

She hadn't been mistaken yesterday; it had been Andy standing outside in the crowd as she went to the wedding. But why did he want to see her...?

CHAPTER ELEVEN

'YOU just aren't thinking this through at all, Lilli,' Patrick said as he sat watching her dress. 'Brewster believes that by talking to you, appealing to your softer nature, he may be able to stop your father's legal proceedings against him!'

She didn't look at him, hadn't done so since he'd followed her into the bedroom a few minutes ago. They had made love in this room, knew each other intimately, and yet she still felt slightly self-conscious at having Patrick watch her, thankfully pulling up the side zip to olive-green trousers before pulling on a matching sweater.

She was still stunned by Andy's contact with her father, couldn't imagine what had made him do such a thing. She certainly didn't agree with Patrick's last comment; she had every reason to hate Andy, and he must be well aware of that fact. Where Andy was concerned, she had no 'softer nature' to appeal to!

'And just how do you think he hopes to achieve that?' she replied, still smarting from Patrick's earlier attempt to tell her what she could and couldn't do. Marriage was a partnership—particularly this marriage!—and she was not about to be told whom she could or couldn't see.

'You were engaged to the man—'

'And he used that engagement to cheat my father,' she reminded him forcefully.

'You loved him—'

'I thought I did,' she corrected him; loving Patrick as

153

she now did, she knew damn well she had never really loved Andy at all!

'You were going to marry him—'

'And now I'm married to you.' She looked at him challengingly. 'A fact I'm unlikely to forget!'

Patrick returned her gaze. 'We made a bargain, Lilli—'

'And I won't renege on that,' she returned sharply. 'But being married to you does not make me your prisoner. I have no idea why Andy wants to talk to me,' she added as his face darkened ominously, 'but I honestly don't see that it can cause any harm.' Her father was right; telling her not to do something was a sure way of ensuring that she did!

Patrick stood up, throwing off his robe, completely unconcerned by his own nakedness as he took underwear from a drawer. 'I'm coming with you,' he informed her as he dressed.

'No!'

He halted in the action of buttoning up his shirt. 'What do you mean…no?' he said slowly.

'I mean no, Patrick,' she repeated firmly, outwardly undaunted by his fury—inwardly quaking. Patrick was again the coldly resilient man who had come to her home the day after their initial night together, a man who seemed like a stranger to her. But she wouldn't allow Patrick to see any of her inner apprehension. 'Andy asked to see me—'

'And I'm now your husband—'

'We aren't joined at the hip, Patrick!' she snapped impatiently. 'And I really don't have the time for this,' she added after glancing at her wristwatch. 'The sooner I see Andy, the sooner we'll all know what's going on.'

'I've already told you what's going on: the man believes he can use emotional pressure, or possibly black-mail—'

'Strangely, I would rather hear all this from Andy himself.' Her eyes flashed deeply green.

Patrick looked at her between narrowed lids. 'You still care for the man...!'

'Rubbish!' Her cheeks were flushed with anger at the very suggestion of it.

In truth, she had come to realise in the last week exactly how shallow her feelings for Andy had been... And it was because she loved Patrick, loved him in a totally different way, completely, intensely, in every way there was to love a man—even his anger!

Andy had been a challenge to her, she had realised, a man who didn't respond to the way she looked as other men always had—for reasons she understood only too well now! But his lack of interest had only piqued her own interest in him a year ago, and it was only since loving Patrick, when every nerve-ending, every part of her, was live to his presence, that she had realised how lukewarm her desire for Andy had been.

To have married him, she now knew, would have been a complete disaster. But she couldn't explain that to Patrick without admitting how she had come to realise that fact. And she couldn't, at this moment, admit to Patrick that he was the very reason she could now see Andy without fear of emotional pressure, of any kind, having any effect whatsoever. Loving Patrick consumed all of her emotions; there was no room for anyone else.

But it was almost as if Patrick's tenderness last night, and again this morning, might never have happened as he continued to glare at her accusingly. Lilli didn't have time to deal with his temper just now, wanted to get this meeting with Andy over and done with.

'Daddy's waiting,' she told Patrick briskly. 'We can talk when I get back—'

'I won't be here, Lilli,' Patrick said flatly.

She gave him a startled look. 'What do you mean…?'

He shrugged. 'By your own words, our honeymoon is over. In which case, I may as well go to my office for a couple of hours.'

For a moment she had thought—! Ridiculous—she and Patrick were married, for life, by his own decree. And, both being determined people, she didn't doubt they would have many disagreements in the future, but that didn't mean either of them intended giving up on their marriage. As Patrick had said earlier, they had made a bargain. For all they knew, she could already have conceived the first of those four children…

Patrick nodded abruptly. 'I'll see you later, Lilli.' He strode out of the room.

No parting kiss, not even a second glance; he just went. And it was with a heavy heart that Lilli joined her father in the suite lounge where he had sat waiting for her.

He looked up, frowning at her. 'Patrick looks—' He hesitated over his choice of description.

'Furious,' she finished for him. 'That's probably because he is.' She slipped on her jacket.

'Actually, I was going to use a much more basic word to describe how he looked,' her father returned ruefully.

She gave a warn smile. 'He doesn't want me to see Andy.'

'I think he made that more than obvious earlier.' Her father grimaced. 'And for once I have to agree with him.'

Her eyes widened accusingly. 'I wouldn't even know

Andy wanted to talk to me if you hadn't come here and told me!'

'I know,' he said wearily. 'And I think now I was probably wrong to do so.'

She laughed dismissively. 'Let's go, Daddy—before you start proving as stubborn as Patrick!' She took a firm hold of his arm and led him out of the suite, locking the door behind them; Patrick had his own key if he returned before them. 'I believe you said Andy wants me to meet him at—' She named a very exclusive hotel as they entered the lift. 'He's staying there on your money, I suppose!' she added scornfully.

Her father raised his eyebrows. 'Who knows? I'm at a complete loss as to what's going on. All he would say when he telephoned earlier was that he had to talk to you—'

'I thought you said he telephoned *you*?' she reminded him.

'I had to say that.' He grimaced. 'How do you think Patrick would have reacted to being told it was you your ex-fiancé wanted—insisted!—on talking to all the time?'

Exactly as he had reacted now—he had walked away!

But she still didn't understand; why did Andy want to talk to her? He had to know how she felt about him now, had to realise that what they had once shared had been over the moment he decided to cheat her father. And used her to do it!

She gave a heavy sigh. 'Maybe we had better not speculate any of this until we see Andy—'

'*You* see him,' her father corrected her. 'He had the damned nerve to tell me he doesn't want to speak to me. Although, to be honest, now that I'm involved in legal proceedings against him, I don't want to speak to him either. I think if I saw him, after the heartache he's caused, I would probably just hit him and think about the consequences of that action later—which wouldn't help anyone! I'll wait outside the hotel for you. But make sure he realises, exactly as I told him on the telephone this morning, that whatever he has to say to you will make no difference to the legal proceedings being brought against him.'

Now she was even more puzzled by this meeting between Andy and herself. He didn't want to see her father... She didn't know what she had been expecting— perhaps a plea from Andy, or even the blackmail that Patrick had suggested. Now she wasn't so sure...

Andy sat alone at one of the tables in the huge reception area, a pot of coffee in front of him. Lilli had time to study him before he was aware of her presence. The last three months hadn't been kind to him either; his handsome face was ravaged and tired-looking, his suit fitting him loosely, as if he had lost weight too.

Lilli hardened her heart to the way he looked; he was the cause of everyone's unhappiness, including his own, from the look of him!

She walked to the table, standing beside it looking down at him wordlessly as she waited for him to say something.

He stood up. 'At least sit down, Lilli,' he said, holding back the chair for her. 'You're looking well,' he told her as he resumed his own seat opposite her.

'What do you want, Andy?'

'I suppose it is a little late for social politeness between us,' he conceded. 'Could I just say, I never meant to hurt you, Lilli—?'

'Didn't you?' she interrupted.

He gave a sad sigh. 'No...'

'You hurt me because of what you did to my father, but on a more personal level…?' She shook her head, her eyes flashing her pain. If she had been hurt in any way by the end of their engagement then it had been her pride that had taken the blow—and, as Patrick had already assured her all too clearly, she had more than enough of that!

Andy looked at her closely for several seconds, and then he slowly nodded. 'I'm glad about that. I thought by the announcement of your marriage to Devlin that I couldn't have done you too much harm—'

'I haven't come here to discuss the harm—or otherwise!—that you did to me,' Lilli cut in. 'My father is the one— What on earth is that?' She stopped as Andy produced a small flat package from his jacket pocket, the paper brightly coloured, decorated with a silver bow and ribbon. 'I realise it's Christmas tomorrow, Andy—' her mouth twisted contemptuously as she looked at the present '—but I—'

'It isn't a Christmas present, Lilli, it's a wedding gift,' Andy told her, holding out the small present to her.

Her eyes widened, her hands tightly locked together in her lap. 'I don't want anything from you!' And she knew, without even consulting him, that Patrick wouldn't want it either!

'You'll want this.' Andy continued to hold out the gaily wrapped gift, but when she still didn't take it he put it down on the table between them, standing up. 'Please tell your father I'm sorry.'

'Where are you going?' she said incredulously as he would have walked away; she still had so much to say to him!

He gave a little smile. 'I'm not going anywhere, Lilli;

I'm staying exactly where I am. The last three months have been a nightmare—'

'You think they've been a nightmare for *you*?' she demanded disbelievingly. 'What do you think it's been like for my father? He—'

'I know,' Andy acknowledged heavily, coming down on his haunches beside her chair, reaching out to clasp both her hands in his. 'I do know, Lilli. That's why I'll understand if, after opening your present, your father still wants to prosecute me.' He shook his head sadly. 'It was all so tempting, Lilli, too much so in the circumstances.' He looked at her pleadingly. 'I was involved in a relationship that—well, I was in over my head. I thought if I had some money of my own—'

'I know about your—relationship, Andy,' she told him hardly. 'It's the reason I know you could never really have cared for me!'

He closed his eyes briefly, those eyes slightly over-bright when he raised his lids to look at her once again. 'I did—do—care for you, Lilli. You're a wonderful woman—'

'Please, Andy.' She instantly shook her head. 'Don't take me for a complete fool!'

He let out a deep breath. 'I know how it must seem to you, but I— If things had been different—'

'Don't you mean, if *you* had been different?' she countered, pulling her hands away from his.

'Yes,' he acknowledged. 'But you really are an exceptional woman, Lilli—a caring, beautiful woman. And you deserved so much better than me—'

'She got it!' interrupted a harsh voice.

Lilli and Andy turned sharply in the direction of that voice, Lilli troubled, Andy guarded, slowly straightening to face the other man. Lilli couldn't even begin to imagine what Andy thought of Patrick's presence here—she was too busy wondering about that herself!

Patrick's mouth showed his contempt as he looked at the younger man. The two were in such stark contrast to each other, Patrick so dark where Andy was golden, Patrick's face masculine, Andy's, seen against such stark masculinity, appearing much softer, his features so regular and handsome he appeared almost beautiful.

As the two men continued to stare at each other, Lilli couldn't help wondering if Patrick had entered the hotel in time to see Andy holding her hands...!

Whatever he had or hadn't seen, his cold anger of earlier this afternoon certainly hadn't diminished; he still looked furious!

'Lilli and I were married yesterday,' he informed Andy icily, pulling Lilli to her feet so that she stood at his side, holding her there firmly, his arm like a steel band about her waist.

Andy nodded. 'I realise that.'

'Then you must also realise that you have intruded on our honeymoon,' Patrick barked. 'An unwelcome intrusion.'

'I realise that too,' Andy acknowledged ruefully. 'But I had something I had to give to Lilli.' He bent down and picked up the gaily wrapped present before handing it to Lilli. 'I hope the two of you will be very happy together,' he added lightly, although he seemed to frown as he glanced at Patrick's harshly set face, his expression softening as he turned to Lilli. 'You're a very lucky man to have Lilli for your wife.' Even as he spoke to Patrick he bent forward and lightly kissed Lilli on the cheek. 'Take care, love. And be happy.' He turned and walked away.

There was complete silence as Andy left the hotel,

Lilli still clutching the small present he had given her,
Patrick silent at her side. She didn't need two guesses
as to why; he was absolutely furious—at her for seeing
Andy at all, but also at the fact that the man had dared
to kiss her, albeit on the cheek!

'For goodness' sake, stop brooding, Patrick!' she told
him spiritedly as she moved out of his grasp. 'I don't
recall that I behaved this way yesterday when your ex-
wife decided to turn up at our wedding!' In fact, that
subject hadn't been mentioned, by either of them, since.

He looked blank, as if the memory was something he
had completely forgotten about. And perhaps it was;
Sanchia didn't appear to be someone he wanted to remember. But that didn't change the fact that his reaction
to Andy now was completely unfair to her.

Patrick relaxed suddenly. 'Let's sit down for a while.
Your father has gone home, so he isn't going to be waiting outside. I spoke to him on my way in,' he supplied
at her questioning look. 'I couldn't see the point in both
of us waiting for you.' The two of them sat at the table
Andy had recently vacated.

Of course not. And, of course, her father would also
have seen the sense of that—with a little help from
Patrick…!

'Open the damned present,' Patrick instructed tersely.
'Although I still think, given the circumstances, that
Brewster had a damned nerve wanting to see you at all,
let alone give you a present!'

Lilli wasn't really listening to him, was staring down
at the gift she had just unwrapped, the silver ribbon and
bow hanging limply from her hand now.

'What is it?' Patrick prompted sharply. 'Lilli!'

She looked across at him, her eyes unfocusing, her
face pale. She couldn't think, let alone speak!

'For God's sake...!' Patrick stood up to come round the table and take the package roughly out of her hand, looking quickly at the contents. 'My God...!' he finally breathed dazedly.

Lilli knew exactly what had caused his astonishment. The same thing that had caused her own... Andy's gift to her was a bank account, made out in her name. For the amount of five million pounds!

The amount he had taken from her father...?

She looked up at Patrick. 'Is that what he owed?'

His expression was grim now. 'More or less,' he grated.

She frowned. 'How much less?'

He shrugged. 'Probably the interest that should have been earned in the last three to four months. Brewster has probably needed that for his living expenses. I doubt your father will mind that, as long as he gets the capital returned to him.'

Lilli was still totally fazed, couldn't believe what had just happened. 'Why do you think Andy did it? Gave it back, I mean.' It was almost like a dream, and if it weren't for that bank account—for five million!—Lilli would have had trouble believing Andy had been here at all.

Patrick threw the bank book and account statement down onto the table, sitting in the chair opposite hers once again. 'I did some checking during the short time I had before coming here. Brewster's relationship has apparently foundered, probably because of the pending court case; his lover is apparently the type who doesn't care to be associated with criminals! So maybe Brewster just decided to try and salvage at least part of his life and try to walk away. I have a feeling your father will let him do that.'

So did she, once she had spoken to her father. 'He's certainly going to be ecstatic at the return of this.' She touched the statement as if she still couldn't believe the money was actually there, within her father's grasp.

Patrick said, 'He's gone back to Gerry's house, if you want to take it to him.'

This time Lilli didn't feel that sickening lurch in her stomach at the mention of the relationship between his sister and her father. Maybe she was getting used to the idea…

'And you?' Patrick suddenly asked her. 'How do you feel about it?'

She gave a glowing smile. 'Wonderful! Daddy has his money back, and it looks as if all the publicity a court case would have engendered can be avoided as well. It's— But you don't look too pleased, Patrick.' She suddenly realised he looked grimmer than ever. 'Do you think there's something wrong with the return of the money?' She looked down at the bank statement. 'Is Andy playing some sort of cruel joke on us all? Do you—?'

'Relax,' Patrick advised. 'The money is in a bank account in your name. It's yours. But it means the two of us have some serious talking to do once you've seen your father,' he added firmly.

Lilli looked startled. 'We do…?'

'One day, Lilli,' he bit out. 'Do you realise that if Brewster had returned that money to you just one day earlier you wouldn't now be my wife?' He looked at her intently. 'Would you?'

All the colour drained from her face as the force of his words hit her. One day… If Andy had come to see her the day before her marriage to Patrick, then he was right—there would have been no wedding. She wouldn't now be Patrick's wife. Never would have been!

She couldn't speak as this sickening realisation hit her.

'Exactly,' he grated, standing up. 'I really do have some things to do at the moment, Lilli. But we'll talk about this later at the hotel.'

Lilli sat and watched him go, her eyes dark green pools. Exactly what were they going to talk about? Not divorce? Did Patrick realise, with the return of this money, that they should never have been married at all? Did none of last night and this morning matter to him? Did he want to end their marriage before it had even begun?

CHAPTER TWELVE

'BUT this is wonderful!' Her father's delight was obvious as he smiled broadly. 'Absolutely marvellous!'

'But is it?' Gerry said slowly, looking at Lilli. 'Lilli doesn't look too happy.'

Her father turned to her too now, noticing the paleness of her face. 'Lilli?' he said warily. 'Brewster didn't say or do anything to upset you, did he?'

'No,' she dismissed with a shaky laugh.

'There aren't any hidden conditions attached to the return of this money, are there?'

She had come in a taxi straight to Gerry's house, knew she had to put her father's mind at rest as soon as possible. But inside she was still in shock from Patrick's enigmatic comments before he'd left her, couldn't actually remember the taxi journey here.

'No hidden conditions,' she assured her father wryly. 'I think Andy was quite relieved to get rid of it; a life of crime doesn't seem to have brought him too much happiness!'

'Then—'

'Where is Patrick, Lilli?' Gerry interjected. 'Richard said he came to join you at the hotel…?'

'He did.' She avoided the other woman's gaze: Gerry saw far too much! 'But he had some business to attend to,' she added brightly.

'Did he?' Gerry returned sceptically.

Lilli still didn't meet her sister-in-law's eyes. 'He said he did, yes.'

'But...?'

'Really, Gerry.' Lilli gave a light laugh, although no humour reached the dull pain in her eyes. 'You know Patrick—if he says he has something else to do, then he has something else to do.'

'I do know Patrick,' his sister acknowledged softly. 'We've always been very close. He more or less brought me up, you know.'

'Yes, he told me about that,' Lilli replied, those moments of intimacy between them seeming a lifetime away.

'Did he?' Gerry nodded her satisfaction with that. 'Then you must realise that the two of us know each other rather better than most brothers and sisters, that we've always had an emotional closeness?'

Lilli gave the other woman a puzzled glance. 'I don't understand where all this is leading to—'

'It's leading to the fact that Patrick is in love with you,' Gerry told her impatiently. 'And I have a feeling— a terrible feeling!—that because of this—' she held up the bank book and statement '—Patrick is going to do something incredibly stupid!'

Lilli was quick to protest, 'Patrick isn't in love with me, and—'

'Oh, yes, he is,' the other woman assured her with certainty.

'—he never does anything "incredibly stupid",' Lilli finished determinedly. 'Unless you count marrying me in the first place,' she added bitterly.

'Lilli, exactly what has Patrick said to you?' Gerry probed.

Lilli stood up and turned away from both her father and the other woman. 'Apart from more or less saying

we should start talking about a divorce?' she said
fiercely. 'Not a lot!'

'A divorce?' her father echoed incredulously. 'But
you were only married yesterday! He can't be serious—'

'They were married yesterday, Richard,' Gerry cut in
gently. 'But today the reason for Lilli marrying
Patrick—that money—' she gestured in the direction of
the bank book '—was made null and void. That is the
reason Patrick believes you married him, isn't it, Lilli?'

She was starting to resent Gerry again; this was none
of her business, even if she was Patrick's sister! '*It is*
the reason I married him,' Lilli came back; she didn't
believe either of these two could seriously have ever
been fooled into believing otherwise!

'So you're going to agree to a divorce?' Gerry
watched her shrewdly.

Lilli felt ill just at the thought of it, knowing she must
have once again gone pale. 'If that's what Patrick's
wants, yes.'

'And what do *you* want?' the other woman persisted.

'You know Patrick; I don't think I'll have a lot of say
in this one way or the other!'

'Lilli, your father told me Patrick said he hadn't raised
a fool.' Gerry spoke plainly. 'But at this moment you're
being extremely foolish!' she added caustically.

'I don't think I asked for your opinion!' Lilli felt deep
resentment.

'And now you're being very rude,' her father said
sternly, moving forward to put his arms about Gerry's
shoulders. 'Gerry is trying to help you—'

'I don't need—or want!—her help,' Lilli told him
forcefully, her hands clenched at her sides at this show
of solidarity from the couple. The last thing she needed
at this moment was to have their relationship pushed in

her face. She felt as if her whole world was falling apart already, without that!

'Calm down, Richard.' Gerry put a soothing hand against his chest as he would have exploded angrily. 'Lilli is hurt and upset—and God knows we all do stupid things when we feel like that! I think it's time, Richard,' she opined slowly, 'that Lilli heard about some of the stupid things I did in the past—don't you?'

He looked down at her uncertainly. 'I—'

'It's time, Richard,' Gerry repeated firmly. 'Unless you want Lilli to make the same mistake I did? Because, believe me, these two are even more stubborn than we are, and at this moment, basically because she's here and Patrick isn't, I think Lilli is more open to reason.'

Lilli's father glanced across at his daughter uncertainly, Lilli steadily returning his gaze. She had no idea what all this was about, and she wasn't sure she wanted to know either. But she did know that when she got back to the hotel Patrick was going to talk about their future— or lack of it!—and anything that delayed that happening was acceptable!

'Very well.' Her father finally gave his agreement. 'But listen carefully, Lilli. And try not to judge,' he added almost pleadingly.

'Do I need to sit down for this?'

'Yes,' her father confirmed, going to the drinks tray on the side dresser. 'You're also going to need this.' He handed her a glass of brandy. 'We all are!' He handed another glass to Gerry, and kept one for himself.

Lilli sat, although she made no move to drink the brandy, putting the glass down on the table beside her chair, looking up expectantly at Gerry.

The other woman looked apprehensive at her sceptical expression. 'Your father is right, Lilli—you aren't going to like what you hear,' she said. 'But please try to understand; this isn't being done to hurt; I'm doing this for an altogether different reason.'

'I'll try,' Lilli conceded dryly.

'Lilli—'

'Leave it, Richard,' the other woman told him lightly. 'Lilli makes no pretence of doing anything other than disliking me, and at least it's honest. It isn't what I would like, but it's honest.' She walked over to the blazing fire, suddenly seeming to need its warmth. 'Six years ago I met a man I fell very much in love with,' she began. 'Unfortunately, the man was married— We haven't all led neatly packaged lives, Lilli,' she added at Lilli's derisive expression. 'The man was married. Unhappily—I know, aren't they all?' she acknowledged self-deprecatingly. 'But in this case it was true. I had seen the two of them together, knew that the wife was involved with someone else. And I—I fell in love with the husband. And he loved me in return.'

'But your marriage only lasted a couple of months,' Lilli pointed out. 'Hardly the love of a lifetime!' she said scathingly, wondering why she was being told all this.

'Because I didn't marry the man I loved!' Gerry returned curtly. 'There were complications. The man had a child. At fifteen, not a very young child, I'll admit, but a child the father loved very much. And there were reasons why—why this man couldn't leave his wife and child.'

'Once again, there always are,' Lilli returned without interest, this was an all-too-familiar story, surely...?

Gerry drew in a harsh breath. 'But in this case the wife threatened to completely alienate the child from the father if he dared to leave her—'

'But I thought you said she was involved in an affair, too?'

'She was,' Gerry rasped. 'And if things had been—different she had intended leaving her husband! But the woman became ill, seriously so, and her—lover decided he didn't want to tie himself to a woman dying of cancer.'

Lilli had become suddenly still, her eyes wide now as she stared at Gerry. 'Go on...'

'Your father and I were deeply in love, Lilli,' Gerry told her emotionally. 'We had intended being together. But he—he left it too late to agree to giving your mother a divorce. She had been diagnosed as terminally ill, her lover left her, and suddenly all she was left with was a broken marriage. And her daughter.' Gerry swallowed hard. 'She was determined to hang onto both of them—at any cost.'

Lilli could hardly breathe, felt suddenly numb.

'Your parents' marriage began to deteriorate after your brother died, Lilli,' the other woman continued huskily. 'Your father buried himself in his work—and loving you. And your mother went from one affair to another. And the love they had once felt for each other turned to a tolerant contempt. By the time I met your father four years later they were living completely separate lives, with you as their only common ground.'

Lilli looked at her father with pained eyes, couldn't believe she could have been so blind to her parents' loveless marriage. Or perhaps she hadn't... She had known they spent little time together, that her mother could be verbally vicious to her father when she chose to be, but she had always put that down to the pain of her illness. Now she could see that perhaps it had been that they simply didn't love each other any more...

'Daddy...?' She looked at him emotionally now.

'I'm sorry, Lilli. So sorry.' He gripped her hands tightly. 'But it's all true. In fact, there's so much more. Your mother had asked me for a divorce before she found out about her illness, was going off with this other man—'

'Richard...!' Gerry looked at him uncertainly.

He shook his head, his gaze still on Lilli. 'It's time it all came out, Gerry. Your mother was leaving us, Lilli. She had told me she was going, asked me for a divorce—on her terms, of course. She wanted a huge settlement of money, and in return she would leave you with me. The man she was involved with was ten years younger than her, and he didn't want Caroline's fifteen-year-old daughter cluttering up their lives.'

'Mummy was leaving me behind,' Lilli said dazedly.

'Yes,' he replied. 'And I was happy to give her the money if I could keep you. Then she found out she had cancer...' His expression darkened. 'And everything changed!'

'Lilli!' Gerry came to her side as she swayed where she sat. 'No more of that, Richard,' she said briskly. 'I only wanted to try to explain a little...'

'I've misjudged you,' Lilli realised flatly, reaching out blindly to clasp the other woman's hand—blindly because her eyes were full of tears. 'Patrick knows all of this, doesn't he?' She realised only too well now what he had meant when he'd said her father had been protective of her to the point of stupidity! She looked up at her father now. 'You gave up your chance of happiness because you didn't want to lose me,' she said brokenly.

'You had already been through so much when we lost Robbie—'

'You gave up the woman you loved—Gerry—' she

looked at the other woman as the tears began to fall down her cheeks '—so that Mummy wouldn't destroy all our lives. And you...' She tightly squeezed Gerry's hand. 'You married someone else on the rebound.' She recalled her father's words... 'An angry and upset Gerry is a force to be reckoned with!'

'Oh, Lilli!' Gerry moved to hug her. 'Don't make the same mistake. Please!'

She pulled back slightly. 'You mean Patrick?'

'I mean my stubborn, arrogant brother,' Gerry confirmed. 'It runs in the family, I'm afraid. Your father went out of my life five years ago because I was too stubborn to listen to him. I married—disastrously—to spite him. I loved him, wanted to be with him, and although I understood what he was doing it was impossible for me to stay in his life. My marriage was a mess, and within a couple of months I had to admit I had made a terrible mistake.' She grimaced at the memory. 'Don't do something stupid like I did, Lilli. I know Patrick; he would never have married you if he didn't love you.'

'When he asked me to marry him it was because he said I had the qualities he wanted in his wife, in the mother of his children—'

'He probably believed it when he said it too.' Gerry shook her head with affectionate exasperation. 'But it's all nonsense. Patrick is in love with you— Yes, he is, Lilli,' she insisted firmly even as Lilli opened her mouth to deny it. 'Do you love him? The truth, Lilli. It's the day for the truth,' she went on throatily.

Lilli took a deep breath. 'I— Yes!' The word was virtually forced out of her. It was one thing to admit to herself how she felt, quite another thing to admit it to someone else. Even someone she realised she had completely misjudged... God, Gerry should have been the one resenting her all this time, not the other way around. So many years wasted… And what Gerry was saying to her now was, did she want to waste as many by giving up on Patrick without a fight? But Gerry had known Richard loved her, whereas Patrick didn't love Lilli at all…

'Then what do you have to lose by telling him so?' Gerry sat back, her expression encouraging. 'Your pride? Oh, Lilli!' She held her hand out towards the man she loved, straightening to stand at his side. 'My pride, after I made such a mess of things, cost me years I could have spent with your father. Long, lonely years, when I went out with lots of men who meant nothing to me, men who, because of their own male pride, would never admit to anyone that those relationships were never physical. I've been so lonely, for so long, without your father, Lilli; but thank God he came back and claimed me once he was free to do so!'

'And—thank God—she let me!' Lilli's father added with feeling.

Lilli smiled shakily up at the two of them. 'So when are the two of you getting married?'

'As soon as you and Patrick agree to be our witnesses,' her father told her.

Patrick… A shadow passed over her face, her smile, emotional as it was, fading.

'I'm ordering you to stay away from him, Lilli,' her father told her expectantly.

Her smile returned, a little wanly, but it did return. 'That won't work this time, Daddy. I—' She broke off as the telephone began to ring, Gerry going to answer it.

'Good afternoon, Patrick,' she greeted once he had identified himself as the caller. 'Richard is ecstatic over

the news, and— Yes, Lilli is still here.' She glanced
across the room at a now tense Lilli. 'Well, we're all
just about to sit down and enjoy a celebratory glass of
champagne— Yes, I know it's your honeymoon,' she
answered him smoothly. 'But it's Christmas too. And
we all have something to celebrate—why don't you
come and join us—?' Gerry suddenly held the receiver
away from her ear, wincing as the loudness of Patrick's
voice down the receiver could now be heard by all of
them, although the words themselves were indistinct.
'Well, it's your choice, of course. Lilli will be back
later.' Gerry looked down at the receiver, shrugging before placing it back on its cradle. 'I'll give him twenty
minutes.' She grinned.

'For what?' Lilli frowned, having been frozen in her
seat since she realised it was Patrick on the telephone,
her hands still shaking slightly.

'For him to get here.' Gerry grinned her satisfaction.
'And you doubted he loves you! Patrick never shouts,
Lilli. He's never needed to. The softer he talks, the more
anxious people are to do what he wants. But he's shout-
ing now, Lilli—and it's because I deliberately gave him
the impression you wouldn't be going back to the hotel
until later this evening.' She laughed, glancing at her
wristwatch. 'Eighteen minutes, and counting!'

Lilli was sure the other woman was wrong. As his
sister, she might know Patrick very well, but she had no
knowledge of him as a husband. There was no way
Patrick would come to her…

And she wasn't going to him yet either, wasn't ready
for that, readily falling in with her father's suggestion
that they have the champagne after all. Anything to de-
lay going back to the hotel. And discussing their divorce…

'To the two of you.' She toasted her father and Gerry
with pink champagne. 'May you be happy together at
last.' She owed them this much, owed them so much
more than she had ever realised.

Her marriage to Patrick meant she was no longer a
child, and she was learning all too forcefully what
Patrick had said all along: things were never just black
and white. No one was to blame for the triangle that had
evolved six years ago, not even her mother. Maybe it
wasn't emotionally fair, but, faced with a sure slow
death, her mother had clung to the things that she still
could, and that included her husband and daughter.
Given the same circumstances, Lilli wasn't sure she
would have done the same thing, but it was what had
happened, and it was over now. It was time to shut the
door on that, and start again.

For all of them, it seemed…

She swallowed down her feelings of apprehension
with the champagne. Time enough to face all that later;
right now was the time to let her father celebrate. And
for him and Gerry to be allowed to be happy with each
other at long last.

'Hmm, three minutes early,' Gerry suddenly murmured after another glance at her watch. 'He must have
broken several speed limits to get here this fast at this
time of the day—and on Christmas Eve!' She smiled
across at Lilli. 'I just heard Patrick's car in the drive-
way.' She listened again. 'Patrick entering the house,'
she added ruefully as the front door could be heard slam-
ming loudly shut. 'Patrick entering the room,' she announced before turning to face him, a glowing smile
lighting up her face. 'Patrick, what a surprise!' she
greeted warmly. 'You decided to join us, after all.'

He didn't even glance at his sister, all his attention

focused on Lilli as she stood near the fire. 'I thought you were coming back to the hotel once you had spoken to your father,' he grated accusingly.

Her hand trembled slightly as she held onto her champagne glass. 'We were celebrating,' she said with soft dismissal.

'Richard and I were just going off in search of another bottle of champagne,' Gerry said lightly. 'Weren't we, darling?' she prompted pointedly.

'Er—yes. We were,' he agreed somewhat disjointedly, frowning at Lilli and Patrick.

Patrick returned his gaze coldly. 'Pink, of course,' he said. 'It's Lilli's favourite.'

'How well you know your wife,' Gerry drawled, lightly touching his cheek as she passed him on her way to the door. 'We shouldn't be too long,' she assured Lilli gently in passing.

The room suddenly seemed very quiet once the other couple had left, closing the door softly behind them, even the ticking of the clock on the fireplace suddenly audible.

Lilli could only stare at Patrick. Dear God, he looked grim. Her hands began to shake again as she tightly gripped the glass.

'But not for much longer, hmm, Lilli?' he suddenly exclaimed as he strode further into the room, dark and overpowering in black denims and a black sweater. 'Will I know you as my wife?' he added at her puzzled frown.

Something seemed to snap inside her at that moment, a return of the old Lilli through the fog of uncertainty, pain, truth—so much truth, it was still difficult to take it all in!—and she faced Patrick unflinchingly as she carefully placed her glass down on the table behind her. 'I thought we had an agreement that our marriage was

for life,' she reminded him haughtily—every inch
Elizabeth Bennett at that moment. But she was neither
Just Lilli nor Elizabeth Bennett any more, she was Lilli
Devlin—and she was about to fight for what she wanted!
'The agreement—verbal though it might have been—
was binding on both sides. You can't just opt out of it
when it suits you, Patrick.' She still didn't believe that
Patrick loved her—it would be too much to hope for!—
but if she could remain his wife, who knew what might
happen in the future…?

'When it suits me—!' he exploded furiously, a nerve
pulsing erratically in the hardness of his cheek. 'It
doesn't *suit* me at all to have my wife walk out on me
the day after our wedding! Even Sanchia waited a little
longer than that.'

'Forget Sanchia,' Lilli returned. 'I am not her, am
nothing like her. And I'm not walking out on you.'

'I have just spent most of the day, the day following
our wedding, at the hotel on my own,' he bit out. 'I
would say that's walking out!'

'Rubbish,' she snapped back. 'I spent all of the morning and part of the afternoon, at the hotel with you,' she
reminded him, a blush to her cheeks as she remembered
those hours of intimacy. 'We've been apart maybe three
hours at the most—'

'And look what happened in those three hours!' he
said disgustedly.

'What, Patrick? What happened during that time?' she
challenged. 'My father had his money returned to him.
What does that have to do with us, with our marriage?
You told me last week that it wasn't mentioned during
the proposal or the acceptance; so what bearing does this
afternoon's events have on our marriage? Well?' she
pressed after several seconds of tense silence.

He gave a snort. 'Everything!'

She became suddenly still, looking at him carefully. 'Why?'

'Oh, for God's sake, Lilli.' He paced about the room. 'It may not have been mentioned, but we both know how relevant Brewster giving the money back is to us; you admitted as much yourself earlier this afternoon when I asked you!'

She thought back to their conversation after Andy had left, to what Patrick had said, because she hadn't said anything! 'And just how did I admit it, Patrick?' she asked softly. 'I don't believe *I* said anything.'

'You didn't have to,' he groaned. 'The look on your face when you realised how close you had come to not marrying me spoke for itself; you went white!'

She drew in a deep breath. Pride, Gerry had told her, had cost her six years of happiness with the man she loved...

'Are you interested in why I went white, Patrick?' she said.

'I know why you went white,' he ground out, glaring at her. 'You missed keeping your freedom by twenty-four hours!'

Lilli steadily met his tempestuous gaze, unmoved by the fierceness of his expression. 'You're partly right—' She ignored his second snort of disgust in as many minutes, choosing her words carefully. 'I realised,' she said slowly, 'how narrowing I had avoided not marrying you—'

'Then we don't have a problem, do we, because—?'

'Be quiet, Patrick, and let me finish what I'm saying!' She glared at him. 'And listen, damn it! I said "how narrowly I had avoided *not* marrying you" —because if Andy had come back into our lives two days ago *you* would have been the one to call off the wedding. Wouldn't you?' she persisted.

'I—'

'Not me, Patrick,' she continued unwaveringly. 'I wouldn't have called it off, because I *wanted* to marry you!' The last came out in a rush, Lilli holding her breath now as she waited for his reaction.

He continued to look at her, but some of the fierceness went out of his expression, uncertainty taking its place.

And uncertainty wasn't an emotion Lilli had ever associated with Patrick before...

'Why?' he said bluntly.

She swallowed hard. Could she really just tell him—? Pride, Gerry had called it. And look what it had cost the other woman in terms of real happiness...!

She drew in a deeply controlling breath. 'Because I love you!' Once again the words came out in a rush, and it was her turn to look uncertain now. 'I know you don't love me,' she continued hurriedly at Patrick's stunned expression. 'That you decided never to love again after Sanchia—'

'As you said earlier—forget Sanchia,' he dismissed harshly. 'As far as I'm concerned she ceased to exist the day she decided to destroy our child because she believed pregnancy would ruin her figure—'

'Patrick, no!' Lilli gasped disbelievingly. How could anyone destroy another human life for such selfish reasons? The life of Patrick's child... Which was why he had asked her if she wanted children... Why he had made such a point of telling her she would look beautiful when she was pregnant...! 'Oh, Patrick...!' Her voice broke emotionally as she went to him, her arms going about his waist as she rested her head against his chest.

'You said you loved me...?' he said quietly.

He stood a little apart from her, his own arms loose at his sides, his expression distant as she looked up at him. 'Not the past tense, Patrick.' She shook her head firmly. 'I do love you. Very much. And I do not want a divorce,' she added determinedly. 'I told you before, you aren't going to have everything your own way—'

'I don't want a divorce either!' His voice rose agitatedly, moving at last, his arms coming tightly about her waist. 'I thought you did. I thought— Lilli, I know what I said to you when I asked you to marry me.' He looked intently down at her. 'I was trying to protect myself, trying—' He shook his head in self-disgust. 'I lied, Lilli. I—'

'You don't tell lies, Patrick,' she reminded him softly, hope starting to blossom somewhere deep inside her, too deep down yet to actually flower, but it was there nonetheless...

'Lilli. Just Lilli. *My* Lilli.' His hands cupped either side of her face as he raised it to his. 'That first night at the hotel, as you lay sleeping in the bed— Don't look like that, Lilli,' he admonished gently. 'You were beautiful that night. I lay beside you for hours just watching you.' He smiled as she looked startled. 'You were— are—so beautiful, and yet as you slept you looked so vulnerable. By the time morning came I had decided I wanted to spend the rest of my life waking up with you beside me. I didn't recognise those feelings as love then, but—'

'Love?' she echoed huskily, that hope starting to flower now, to grow and grow, until it filled her.

'Love, Lilli. I fell in love with you that night. Although I certainly didn't recognise it as such.' He grimaced. 'Only that I wanted you with me for the rest of my life. But when I came out of the bathroom that morning you had gone...'

'I felt so embarrassed by what I had done.'

'I realise that,' he nodded. 'It was the shock of my life, only a matter of hours after that, to discover you were actually Richard Bennett's daughter. With all the complications that entailed—'

'I know about my mother, Patrick,' she interrupted. 'And about Gerry and my father. I— We've all made our peace.'

'Have you? I'm glad. Gerry's life was such a mess five years ago, and for years I harboured very strong feelings against your father for causing that unhappiness. And then two months ago Gerry took him back into her life, and I— I didn't take the news too well initially. Maybe I was a bit over-zealous—businesswise—where your father was concerned, because of that. Part of me wanted him destroyed in the way he had destroyed my sister's life,' he admitted heavily.

'And you hated me because I was his daughter,' Lilli said knowingly.

'I didn't hate you.' His arms tightened about her once again. 'I could never hate you. I was not—pleased to discover you were his daughter.'

'You believed I had slept with you deliberately,' she reminded him teasingly.

'Only for a matter of a few hours. I was so damned angry when I found out who you really were that it seemed the only explanation for the way you had left the party with me—'

'I had just seen my father with Gerry,' she told him. 'I was angry and upset, and although I didn't know you were Gerry's brother the two of you seemed close, and so I—I decided to go with you to spite her. Not very nice, I'll grant you, but at the time I just wasn't thinking straight. I got the shock of my life when I woke up that morning in a hotel bedroom and heard you singing in the adjoining bathroom!'

'Well, of course I was singing,' he grinned. 'I had just found the woman I wanted to spend the rest of my life with!'

'And I thought I had spent the night making love with you and couldn't even remember it!' she recalled with a groan.

'I know, love,' he said. 'That was obvious when I came to your house later that day.'

'And you let me carry on believing it!' she reproved exasperatedly.

'Don't be too angry with me, Lilli.' He kissed her gently on the lips. 'It was the fact that we hadn't made love that made me realise I had made a mistake about that. When I sat and thought about it later, if you really had set out to trick me that night, you would never have allowed yourself to go to sleep in the way that you did, and you certainly wouldn't have left the hotel so abruptly. I also realised, as I sat angrily churning all this through my mind, that our night together actually made things less complicated rather than more so. It enabled me to ask you to marry me,' he explained at her questioning look, 'to point out all the advantages of such a marriage, without ever having to admit how I felt about you. I didn't want to love anyone, Lilli, but— What I feel for you is like nothing I have ever known before. I want to be with you all the time. To make love with you. To argue with you—we do them both so well!' He smiled. 'I've never felt like this before, Lilli,' he told her intently. 'I love you so very much.'

She believed him! Patrick loved her. And she loved him.

And if either of them needed any further proof of that then the kiss they shared was enough, full of love and aching passion—enough to last a lifetime.

Lilli's eyes glowed, her cheeks were flushed, her lips bare of gloss, when she looked up at him some time later. 'Would you really have let me go?' she prompted huskily.

He frowned. 'If it was what you wanted,' he said slowly.

No, he wouldn't. She knew him too well already to actually believe that. 'Without a fight?' she teased.

'No,' he admitted dryly.

She laughed softly, hugging him tightly. 'I'm so glad you said that—because I wouldn't have gone without kicking and screaming either!'

His answering laugh was full of indulgent joy. 'We're never going to part, Lilli. I'll do everything in my power to make you happy.'

'Just continue to love me,' she told him. 'It will be enough. I—'

'Can we come back in yet?' Gerry looked cautiously around the door she had just opened. 'Only the champagne is getting warm!'

'Do come in.' Lilli held her hand out towards the other woman. 'Let's drink the champagne and make a toast.' She smiled glowingly at her father as he came in carrying the tray with the champagne bottle—pink, of course!—and another glass. 'To a wonderful Christmas and New Year for all of us,' she announced as they all held up their glasses, sure in her heart that every year was going to be a happy one from now on. For all of them.

'How could you do this to me?' Patrick groaned tragically. 'I'll never survive!'

Lilli laughed at his comical expression, very tired, but filled with a glow that shone from deep inside her. 'You'll survive only too well,' she said knowingly. 'Now there will be three of us to love and spoil you.'

'Twins!' Patrick looked down into the cribs that stood next to the hospital bed, gazing in wonder at the identical beauty of the babies that slept within them. 'And both girls,' he added achingly. 'I'm going to end up spoiling all of *you*!'

Lilli smiled at him indulgently. Their daughters had been born fifty-five and fifty-one minutes ago, respectively, and Patrick had been at her side the whole time she had been in labour. As he had been at her side during the whole of the last year...

Lilli had been right; this past year had been the happiest of her life. And she knew it had been the same for Patrick, that the birth of their beautiful daughters on New Year's Eve had made it all complete.

'Think how poor Daddy felt.' She gave a happy laugh. 'James Robert was born on Christmas Day!' No one, it seemed, could have been more surprised than her father when Gerry had presented him with a son a week ago.

It was probably the celebrating that had been going on ever since the birth that had brought on Lilli's own slightly premature labour. But it hadn't been a difficult birth, and their darling little girls were worth any pain she might have felt.

'Now all we have to do is think of names for them both,' Patrick said a little dazedly.

He was right. They hadn't even known she was expecting twins, and because they had been absolutely convinced the baby she carried was a boy they hadn't chosen any girls' names at all.

'Is there room for three more in there?' Her father stood in the doorway, his baby son in his arms, Gerry at his side. 'Or are the Devlins taking over?' he added teasingly.

Lilli's family was complete as her father, Gerry and her new little brother came into the room.

Since she and Patrick had admitted their love for each other, Lilli had been convinced that every new day was the happiest of her life. But as she looked at all her family gathered there together, all so happy, she knew this was definitely their happiest day. Yet...

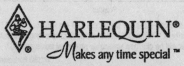

Take 2 bestselling love stories FREE

Plus get a FREE surprise gift!